RINGING
IN A
NEW YEAR

RINGING IN A NEW YEAR

J.K. NORRY

Ringing in a New Year

www.SuddenInsightPublishing.com
Indie publishing for the Indie Author

I.

Studying this body's face in the mirror, I try on a smile. It looks fake, and vaguely nightmarish, so I let the unfamiliar features relax. The ringing is dull and distant, and I put it out of my mind for now. Memories fade like gossamer strands of drifting smoke as I feel my thoughts settle into this mind. There's that thing I need to remember, and I know talking about it will help. I reach for my bell, and forget to make this body breathe for a few moments.

It's gone, and now the memory is too. An even more vague recollection strikes me, that I didn't have my bell in the last body either. It's a thread, and I follow it circuitously through the clogged channels of this sluggish brain. I've almost got it, something important about a body, when a loud voice startles me back into breathing again.

"Please prepare to disembark," the voice says. It's female, but not distinctly so; the distinction is in her clipped but friendly intonation, and her careful enunciation of each word. The voice is coming over a hidden speaker, and draws me back into the room like it drew me back into this body's hitched breathing cycle.

Looking around, I wonder what kind of vehicle this is, to have such stately accommodations. There are no windows, which leads me to believe that it's an inside cabin on whatever vessel this body is in. All other indicators point to luxury, from the thick soft carpeting to the finely stitched linens. At first glance, it could be a five star hotel room in a space made four star by the lack of view; a second glance reveals that everything is definitively affixed to the floor.

Must be a ship, although I can't feel the floor shifting beneath me. The ocean is a hard thing not to feel underfoot, no matter how big the vessel. I don't know why I know that, just that I do. That's the kind of knowledge I get to draw from, either memories that I have somehow tapped into from this body's brain or recollections from my own consciousness filtered through this mind's senseless sensibilities.

For better or worse, I'm used to it.

It's part of being a ringer.

There seem to be few personal items in the room, and I have little use for any of them. It does leap to my attention that the clothes hanging from this body are not fine in either the fit or the form department. I'm delighted to find a selection of suits in the closet, and a garment bag hanging alongside them. I put one on, and place the other two in the bag in a way that will hopefully wrinkle them as little as possible. I may have some unusual abilities, as a ringer; they do not include the ability to be rid of wrinkles in clothing. Skin I can do, as long as it's the skin I'm wearing.

I'm not carrying any more than that, so I leave the suits that won't go with the shoes I choose. When I pat my pockets, they are naturally empty; the phone and wallet that I was carrying were discarded with the pants I'd had on. I kneel to pick them up, find myself surprised that there are two phones in the pockets, and the door opens.

A woman walks into the room, in a pretty sharp uniform of some sort. There are wings on her lapel, with her name under them. I read it aloud.

"Chloe?"

She starts, and exclaims. Something like, "oh!"

"Just finishing packing up," I say.

I'm kneeling still, and smiling.

She looks at the pile of clothes on the floor with the same measure of distaste with which I am handling them. I've got the wallet in my hand now, and I've just pocketed the second phone.

Fully expecting her to excuse herself, and preferably apologize, I'm a little annoyed when she continues to watch me fish around in the worn slacks. Then it hits me, at the same moment she speaks.

"Where is Russell?" she says.

My breathing changed right away; first to calm her, and next to see what she was needing from this exchange. I could see the colors swirling around her energy centers, although they were muddled and blurred. There seemed to be more blue and green going on than any shade of red, so I took a chance.

"I saw you two exchange a friendly word earlier," I said, slipping the phone in one pocket and the wallet in another. I stood up, kept talking.

"I must admit," I shrugged, "I asked him if you two were together, or if you had anybody."

Her eyes went wide, as I had predicted. She leaned away, and looked down at his crumpled pants with that same look of distaste she had twisted her lovely face up with earlier. They were not an item.

I went on.

"He told me you two were going to meet here, in my room," I said.

I looked for the reason in the colors, but couldn't see it. Glancing around the room, I guessed.

"For a drink."

She shook her head, and I nearly started backpedaling.

"It's not your room," she said. "Not anymore."

"Of course." I was the picture of agreeable.

"You were going to meet here," I said, "in this room, after the…"

I eyed her name tag again, guessed again.

"After the flight," I said, nodding.

She nodded along, perplexed at my hesitation.

"For a drink." I kept nodding. I almost had her.

"I asked him," I said, drawing out my words slowly so I could insert his name if I remembered it, "if I might take his place and have that drink with you instead."

Her head kept on tilting in the positive, and I kept this body's head doing the same.

"So…" I gestured at the bar, sure I had her. "How about a drink?"

Suddenly, she stopped nodding.

"Where is Russell?" she demanded. "Why did you take his phone and his wallet? Who are you?"

II.

The deliberate breathing had done more than calm us both down for a moment; it had energized this body as well. It's always disappointing to ring in a healthy specimen and then find its muscles starving for oxygen. With strength comes speed, such that she barely had time to register my movement before I had her.

Sweeping her off her feet in the only way I would apparently be able to, I covered her mouth as her head struck the carpeted floor. For some reason I think of how easily people get knocked out in movies as I hear the soft thud. No actual scenes came to mind, and in the moment I couldn't have named a single title to save this body's life. She was still conscious, of course; so I kept my hand over her mouth and pinched her nose shut with my other hand.

If she had been breathing properly before I cut off her air supply, it probably would not have been so quick. I shift this body's breathing as I look for a place to put what used to be her body. The air churns with energy, colors shift and kaleidoscope in unpredictably ordered patterns, and a streaming seam of electric blue shows me a rectangle nearby.

They're not doorways to other worlds insomuch as they are pockets of otherworldliness. Ringers can't travel to any of those places that souls go after separating from a body, and from what I know I wouldn't want to. Of course, I don't know what I remember; and I don't remember what I know… so I may not be the best entity to consult on such matters.

I do know about hidden spaces between worlds, though. They are simple enough to see, once you get a body's energy flowing properly. I don't know if your typical mortal could open such a doorway once they see them, but I'm neither typical nor mortal.

It comes open easily, a body spills out, and I remember.

I had been trying to imprint this body's mind with old memories, and make mental note of where I had put the fellow I had just finished ringing. That had led to looking for my bell, which I didn't have for some reason. I pat my pockets reflexively, and keep my breathing under control in an attempt to keep the inevitable panic at bay. This leads to the thought that maybe he has my bell for some reason, and next thing you know I'm wrestling one dead body on top of another in exactly the opposite order I should have been.

Turning him over, I searched his pockets. Another wallet, and that's it. I traded it out for the one I had taken from Russell after I compare one body's accoutrements with another's.

Sure; now I remember his name, when it can't possibly help.

My eyes fell on the bar just as the speaker erupted with another announcement.

"All remaining passengers," it said, "please disembark."

It was the same voice as before, a few degrees more clipped and less friendly. I shrugged and ditched the inferior phone that would be of as little use to me in this body as the other wallet. I stuffed him unceremoniously into the small space of timelessness, and piled her on top of him. They looked peaceful together, and kind of sweet.

There was a swirl of darkness as I moved them, and I swear a ghostly skull hovered around me the whole time. I waved it away, and cursed at it under my breath, until it drifted away or dissipated. I closed the door, shifted my breathing and picked up the wardrobe bag. After one last wistful glance at the bar, I pushed open the door that presumably led to the rest of the world.

In the same moment that I stepped into the hallway, the electronic device in my pocket started to buzz and make a noise that made me want to curse the system itself.

First they make a communication device that rings, then they ruin the most compelling part of the device. Old telephones had actual bells in them, activated by an alternating current riding the line of a direct current system, and the sweet sound of dissonance could be heard across the country. Now, even the ones that sound like bells are obvious digital recreations of a noise that could only be called ringing.

It's like pumping false engine noise through stereo speakers because people think that powerful engines should be loud. Really more of an insult to the engines of yesteryear, than anything.

I slip one of this body's hands into the pocket while I return a flight attendant's dirty look with a wide and awkward smile. A quick glance at the screen interrupts my steady breathing altogether, and I feel the smile fall from the unfamiliar features I'm calling my face today.

The incoming call is all nines.

The numbering plan area code is nine-nine-nine.

The central office code is nine-nine-nine.

The line number code is the same, except four nines.

I make this body catch its breath, and see words above the numbers.

'Administration calling...'

Declining the call, I stow the phone in the suit pocket again. I wonder what all that nonsense about the number codes was, cluttering up this brain's limited storage space with trivialities. Grinning at the woman with the wings on her lapel once more, I breeze past her and through the open door. It's a bit of a shock to find that I'm stepping onto the tarmac, and another to realize that there is no security to rifle through this body's things. A man in a black and white suit steps up to me, and reaches out his hand.

Flustered for a minute, I reach out as well. While I'm shaking his hand, I read the confusion on his face and disengage quickly. I hand him my bag, and stride away.

"Let's go, then," I call over my shoulder.

"Sir," he said. "The car is the other way."

III.

There was an opaque sheet of glass between us, which I preferred for the first few minutes. I found that the wireless device I had taken possession of was tuned in to the very fingerprint pattern that I had swirled this body's fingers into. It opened up at my prolonged touch, and showed me a screen full of options in the form of colorful icons. One of them was unusual, pulsing and somehow three dimensional on the flat screen. This time I kept this body breathing, even when I saw that the symbol was a tiny bell. It was too cute to be terrifying, a miniaturized tower bell with a single crack up its dark iron side.

I tapped the banking folder. It opened up, verifying the swirls, and I let this body's heart beat faster. Those long strings of numbers were not negative balances, and there were four other bank icons in the folder. I tried to visualize the possibilities, rather than picture the bell again in this undisciplined mind. It was to no avail, as I had predicted.

The rusted crown, from the moisture that had gathered and clung over the years; the lines of oxidation dripping down the shoulder in thick swaths, and trickling further along the waist in thin scant discolored traces. It had been my favorite kind of image, simple and complex all at once, down to the single crack that ran from the lip to the bead line and just beyond.

Well, that can't possibly be right; surely my favorite kind of image is more compelling than that one, and more arousing in some pleasant fashion.

The thought gives me a laugh, the rising panic subsides, and the image of a rusted and cracked bell slips from this body's mind at last.

Exiting out of one bank app, I check on another. I thank the system for fingerprint technology, and then for the numbers that pop up. I rap on the glass with the phone, wait a second, and do it again.

The partition moves down, and he is looking at me in the rearview through dark sunglasses.

"Sir?" His eyes find the road again.

"Take me to the bank," I say, with utmost confidence.

"Sir?" he says again. "Which bank?"

I shrug. "The one I usually go to."

It's hard not to make it a question, but I do my best. It's also difficult not to feel his eyes on me again, and I straighten this body in its seat.

"Business, sir?" he asks. "Or personal?"

I wave my hand.

"Whichever is closest."

I'm trying to seem irritable, instead of nervous. He's a big guy, and I get the feeling that his skills don't end at driving. The last thing I need is my own security detail suspecting me of not being the person that generally sports this particular face.

"Sir?" His eyes are on me again. "Are you alright?"

It's a simple thing for me to conjure up the rage, when I need to. It's not easy, to forget everything you know on a regular basis and live in swirling confusion for what may as well be eternity. The system needs me, and the system makes sense; but that's intellectual knowledge, and it takes more than that to chip away at the rage.

I let it fill this body's eyes, tense its shoulders and furrow its brow. It seems to fill the spacious back seat, spilling palpably over the lowered glass and into the cab. I can't see his eyes go wide behind his glasses, but I know they do. I let him baste in the bile for a long moment before I speak again.

"Take me to the bank," I say, ice dripping from this body's voice.

I gesture at the sheet of glass.

"And put that back up."

He nods, his hands gripping the wheel while his heart surely pounds in his chest. It takes him a few seconds of fumbling, but he finally manages to separate us.

I'm laughing now, even if it seems a little cruel. When can one be cruel, without harm, if not when one is alone?

When we pull up to the curb, I exit the vehicle without waiting or saying a word. I'm assuming this guy works for me, and that works for me. I know that I can't withdraw more than ten thousand dollars without raising some red flags, and I also know that the law stating so was enacted in 1970. Somehow there is an inflation calculator in this brain, and some silly need to do the math. It informs me, quite uselessly, that I should legally be allowed to withdraw over sixty thousand of those United States dollars. At the level of trust that the government gave its citizens in those days, coupled with the inflation caused by the way they handled the nation's money, the current population is reduced to about the equivalent of fifteen hundred bucks worth of withdrawal or deposit trust.

It barely pads my pocket, and doesn't even come with a fancy band like you see in the movies.

Geez, this guy must have watched a lot of movies. Of course there's no band; I only withdrew ninety one hundred dollar bills. You don't get a band until you hit a hundred, and that's when the man gets involved.

So I take my envelope, my nice suit and this body back to the car. As soon as I tell him that we need to go to another bank, he starts to give off warning signs.

He's knows something is up.

Looks like I'll be driving myself soon.

IV.

There weren't any doorways nearby, so I had to put the body in the trunk. I kept waiting for someone to call out, as I dragged him out of the car and into the street. He went for his gun, and I went for his throat; it all happened pretty quickly, all things considered. The street was neither empty nor full, and no one bothered to even cast a glance in the direction of our struggle. I cleaned up the blood, patched up this body, and hefted him into the back of the car. When I closed it behind him, there was still no one interested in what I was doing.

All of the bank icons had location links, and it was easy enough to find the next closest one. The date icon kept grabbing at my attention, until I reminded this body that the date is always a surprise to a ringer. Everything seems incredibly advanced and ridiculously far behind at the same time, from the immortal perspective. Scenes of finding wall calendars or asking people the year play across the inside of this body's eyes, but it's hard to tell if they are my experiences or just more movies that this guy watched. It doesn't matter, anyway; and I stop checking to drive better.

It's weird, the same drifting amorphous skeletal vision showed up when I was stowing the body. I had to wave it away again, and even swear at it a little, before it would float away. Very disconcerting.

I don't know if they're my memories or this body's cellular recollections or more movies telling me so, but I'm reminded of a time when checking bank balances and locating a branch were much more difficult things. I muse that perhaps the difficulty of life has deflated as much as the economy has inflated as I withdraw another nine thousand of those precious dollars, and consider that maybe modern Americans should only be trusted with what a seventies character would value at about fifteen hundred dollars. With life so easy, they have to make something hard.

While withdrawing the last handful of cash, I reconsider. Interest rates were higher on savings back then, and lower on lending. Plenty of jobs were still available that made it possible for one parent to stay home with kids, and ten thousand dollars would buy you three new cars. If no one is making a fuss about being badgered for carrying that kind of dough, it's likely that very few people are carrying around that kind of dough.

Now that we've established that twenty-seven thousand dollars doesn't exactly make this body wealthy by today's standards, it's a good time to consider what I might be able to do with the money.

The bank parking lot seems a good place to go internal, so I lock the doors and tilt the seat back a bit. I calm this body's breathing, and close its eyes.

I pick up on the ringing right away, and it's as dull and distant as before. An immortal lifetime of forgotten experience tells me that I have a month or so to find whoever is on the other end of that sound and ring them in. I remember the date that shocked me earlier, and let a smile spread across this body's face. It's easier than before, and feels more natural. I let the smile get a little ghastly as I open these eyes and meet them in the rearview.

It looks like I'll be ringing in a new year.

Planning a party will mean putting together some semblance of a life, and it may as well be close to whomever I'll be ringing. It's not easy for this body to breathe right and drive all at the same time, and I discover that pretty quickly. After I've moved the vehicle far away from the ones I damaged, I park it under a tree in hopes that the shade will keep the body from getting too stinky too fast. I make myself a promise that no one else will die at this body's hands, unless you count whoever I have to ring.

Just driving around for a little while made me aware of the fact that this is not a cab city. I'll have to call one, and wait for it, and I probably shouldn't be picked up anywhere close to the corpse that will soon be rotting in the shade.

The thought comes to mind, that I could always kill the taxi driver, and I have to remind myself that there will be no more killing.

For some reason that kicks off a giggling fit that I can't stifle, and I set off walking briskly away from the car while this body's shoulders shake with it. I remember the suits fifty yards away, and it starts off another round of nefarious snickering. I reign in my mind and the giggles as I approach the trunk, remembering both its macabre contents and the fact that I locked the keys in the car.

I'm a ringer, and that's serious business; whatever head I'm occupying, I've got to do my best to keep it on straight. Of course, locks open at my touch, like most folks that are less or more than human. That's not the point, though. I've got to appear as though I'm taking my business seriously if

I want to be taken seriously, and I try on a more suitable laugh as I walk away from the vehicle again.

There will be no more twisted giggle fits, and no more killing.

Unless it's appropriate, of course.

V.

It was easy to breathe right with someone else doing the driving. I was fully aware of the fact that the driver thought I was nodding in and out of some kind of drug stupor between our exchanges, and that he didn't care. I wasn't about to explain to him that I was using my own internal navigation system to find what I was looking for, any more than I was going to kill him. I just let this body's eyes open from time to time, to meet his in the rearview.

As soon as I got in, I pointed.

"That way," I said. "Is there a freeway that goes that way?"

He nodded.

"Yeah, sure," he said. "Eighty goes that way. How far?"

Settling into the seat, I let this body's eyelids drift closed while I breathed. I reached out, felt for the other end of the sound.

"Not far," I said. "Ten miles, maybe fifteen."

"What exit?"

The car hadn't started moving yet, and I was feeling a little annoyed. Not kill someone annoyed, but maybe considering it. I pulled a bill from the bulging stack in the suit pocket and passed it over the seat to him.

"I'll know it when I see it," I said. "If we get going now, I won't be asking for any change."

The hundred disappeared, and now I only had twenty-six thousand, nine hundred dollars. It really should be quite a party.

On the freeway, I breathed my way into sedated silence. The rage subsided, and I saw all thoughts of killing flee from the sudden brilliant burst of internal light. We were getting close, and I opened this body's eyes.

"Not this exit," I said. "The next one."

"Douglas?" His eyes looked back from the rearview. "Or Sunrise?"

I shrugged, and pointed.

"Whichever one goes that way."

There was no reason for me to imagine what I was imagining, as his eyes kept glancing at me in the mirror. I calmed my breathing, dismissed the thought, and let this body's eyelids droop heavily.

"How far down Sunrise, then?"

His gruff voice roused me, and I realized that he may have been alive when a hundred dollars meant something. I had handed him fifteen dollars in yesteryear's currency.

I opened this body's eyes.

"Not much further," I said. "It will be a left turn."

The car changed lanes, quickly but smoothly. I let this body's eyes drift closed once more.

"Alright," I said. "There's a major intersection coming up..."

"Cirby?" He was glancing up again.

"Sure," I said. "Take a left there."

He sighed, in an exaggerated enough fashion that I would see it.

"We're close," I assured him. "Another left, into that housing development."

"You know where you are now, then?" He was smirking,

trying to catch my attention in the rearview.

"I always know where I am," I answered brusquely. "This is your turn."

Under this body's breath, after, I murmured, "I don't ever really know who I am, but I always know where I am."

"What's that?" He was glancing up, and back at the road.

"I think you need to take a right up here," I said.

He chuckled. "Lost again?"

I pressed this body's hands against the glass suddenly.

"See that house?" My words were spoken with wonder.

He tapped the brakes, and started to pull to the curb.

"No, no, keep driving." I waved him away, but kept looking at the house. "It's just a nice house."

The laughter that echoed back at me from the cab of the vehicle had a tinge of cruelty to it, and I finally let him meet this body's eyes in the rearview. It was a special kind of pleasure to watch him shrink visibly, and look away. I do so hate cruelty.

"It's a housing development, that's all," he said meekly. "The homes all look the same."

I patted the seat in front of me, and he flinched away from the movement. It was all I could do not to paint that ghastly smile on this body's face as I pointed one last time.

"There it is," I said. "The place with the sign out in front, saying it's for sale. That's my buddy's house. I remember now."

He pulled to the curb, and parked a little cockeyed and into the street. I couldn't blame him; I probably shouldn't have turned it on so darkly. I thought of giving him another hundred dollar bill, but I honestly didn't feel that much for the guy. Without telling him so, I was doing him a favor by not killing him.

Rather than press me for the money I didn't plan to give him, the driver moved quickly to the back to get my garment bag. It was nice to know that this body would have some decent suits between now and the new year.

Now, I need to see about a house.

VI.

As soon as I ring the doorbell, I hear the pounding of footsteps inside. I'm assessing the lawn with an appreciative eye when the door swings inward, and I stay deliberately turned toward the greenery.

"Nice lawn," I say. "You taking care of the house too?"

He looked befuddled when I finally swiveled and met his eye.

"It is for sale, right?" I made a sweeping gesture with this body's hand. It took in the grass, and ended on him.

"Oh." He nodded. "Yeah, of course. Did you call the agent?"

Having a big strong body is always nice, especially when I get it breathing better. It was nothing to push past him, and make my way inside. The physical contact soothed him, even as it brushed him back, and he let himself be calmed by my presence instead of alarmed by it. He followed me from the closeted split level entrance to the expansive living space.

"Wow," I said, looking around. "You really set it up nice in here. I like the way you divided the area with the sectional, and that television is huge. It's hooked up to the audio system, right?"

"Uh, yeah," he shrugged. "That's our stuff. It's going with us."

It was hard to tell if he caught the fact that I was forcing my laughter to be light, or that I clapped him on the back in the most deliberate way.

"Of course," I said, then continued as he nodded, "we can work something out."

He stopped nodding, and I clapped him on the back again.

"Isn't that right..." I wheedled my way into his thoughts. "Zach?"

At the sound of his name, he relaxed. It doesn't always work, but it works often enough to try it nearly every time. They say everyone's favorite word is their own first name, and it rings true in most cases.

"Well," he said, considering. "We are looking for a fresh start."

I kept walking around, looking at their things.

"No kids, huh?" I noted the cleanliness of the spaces, the lack of toys and stains and lingering frenetic energy patterns.

Zach shook his head, and his youthful features became worn and haggard all of a sudden.

"Not yet," he said.

His eyes found the floor, and his foot traced nonexistent patterns in the plush carpeting. I hadn't noticed that he was holding himself upright until his posture went lax, or that his shoulders were broad and muscled until they sagged. With a shrug, he met this body's eyes.

"We've been trying," he said.

The bitter laugh that followed his statement spoke of volumes that I had absolutely no interest in hearing. I thought it best to keep things on track.

"Is that why you're selling the house, then?" I asked.

I let this body's eyes roam the space once more, ignored his childish foot play on the carpet.

"It seems plenty big enough to start a family in," I said.

His foot stopped moving, finally, but his eyes were locked on the floor again. This time he spoke without looking up.

"It is," he murmured. "That's why we bought it. A half dozen couples that we know live in the developments around here, and some of them had kids when we moved in."

He looked up, frowning.

"They all have kids now," he said. "Everyone but us."

Resisting the urge to tell him that I couldn't care less about the problems his mind had chosen to manufacture for him to test himself against, I tried to lead him back to an adult conversation.

"That still doesn't tell me why you're moving," I pointed out.

He shrugged. This guy did that way too often. I wondered if I had read somewhere that it's a sign of a lack of confidence to shrug so much, or if I had just made it up. Sounds right, either way.

"Kendra got an offer in San Jose," he said. "It's a fresh start, and there are some of the best in vitro fertilization doctors in the country there. We're going to—"

It seems like the perfect opportunity to launch myself at Zach, him being right in the middle of his pathetic rehearsed diatribe. The guy is fast, though; and he grabs both of this body's hands at the wrists way before I wrap its fingers around his throat. Pain shoots up one of the arms that I am inhabiting, and it twists and bends before I have time to dampen this body's organic sensory circuits. This body's face is momentarily buried in that plush carpeting I had been admiring from a standing position a minute ago, and its arm is behind me somewhere.

Zach is on top of me, with his knee in this body's back.

The pain is gone, since I don't wish to feel it; but there is really no point of leverage for me to take advantage of.

"Well," I say, "this is awkward."

He's breathing heavy, and I can hear his heart pounding without manipulating this body's breathing or even closing its eyes. I do need to control my breathing, though, if I'm to turn the tide here.

"I don't know what you're up to," Zach says, all loud and huffy, "but you picked the wrong house, buddy. I wrestled in high school, and I study jujitsu. I could break your arm right now, if I wanted to."

There's a slight movement along my back, and I realize that he is twisting this body's arm even further. Apparently Zach is trying to make a point, and illustrate his words. He twists until there is a pop, but he doesn't get any kind of satisfying wince out of me. Turning this body's frame and face around is no easy task, but I manage it after a few more awkward moments. With my breathing under control, and his all over the place, I catch his eye out the corner of the one I'm looking out of.

"Go ahead," I say, all venom. "Break it."

VII.

He did break this body's arm, but not until a few minutes later. That first shocking look was like a blow, and tossed him back stunned. I got on top of him, and went for his throat again. He pulled that same damned move, and tried to pivot me around on top of him. That's when this body's arm broke, and a moment later he was on its chest again.

When he went for this body's throat, I let him. Zach's fingers dug into it in all kinds of interesting combinations, and he kept watching this face to see it go to sleep. The whole time I watched him back with a detached kind of curiosity, cocking my head to the side in mockery when his hands weren't in the way. This body had been breathing pretty well for awhile now; even if it hadn't, there was no way to put it to sleep while I was in it. I let him try, while I healed the broken arm, and then I let the results of all that breathing flood this body.

It didn't matter what kind of move he threw on me, then. You can't wrestle a hydraulic machine, or someone with the strength of one. One of his arms got broken too, although I couldn't name the method I used to break it. After that, it was pretty quick. Zach had been breathing so badly, once I did get ahold of him it was lights out. I held the hold for quite awhile after he stopped moving, but only because I'm aware of how often people come back to life if you don't drain their fluids or burn them right away.

You know, like polite society's law dictates.

While I let the blood flow into the bathtub and washed it down the drain, that ghastly skull face came drifting into my elevated vision once more. Shooing it away was not nearly as effective as it had been before, and I ended up chasing it down the hall while screaming at the top of this body's lungs. Right in the middle of the chasing and screaming, I wondered if it was some internal vision that signaled my impending insanity. I remembered hearing or saying something about ringers getting cracked, and that once cracked they never ring true anymore.

The vision disappeared in that moment, coincidentally, and I set the line of thought aside. When I was out on the front lawn taking down the sign, I thought I might go back to it. Going back, I found it was no longer there. Instead I thought about how ringers may be individually as old as time, or young as a freshly washed soul. We're certainly the only ones who might possibly be both, as we lose ourselves in one identity after another as the only route to being who we are.

Rather than lament lost memories or wrap myself in the cloying energy of new ones, I wave at a neighbor that's going out to get her mail. She waves back, and I thank the system for the little things.

Back in the house, I find it almost automatic at this point to shift this body's breathing to look for a doorway. As luck would have it, there is one nearby. I don't even have to drag the body outside, and it's not long before I'm settling energetically into my new house. A few framed photographs have to come down, but there aren't even enough to fill the trash bin. Most of the decor is tasteful and well placed, and I am happy to leave it up.

A song starts playing at some point, muted enough for me to think that it is in this body's head for a moment. Then it loops around, and starts again, and I realize it's coming from somewhere in the house. I listen intently, finally, and it stops.

The tussle with Zach damaged this body's suit, and I am annoyed when I notice it. Right there in the middle of admiring the lush master bath, I turn and see this body in the well lighted mirror space. There are seams showing where they shouldn't be on both sleeves, and one of the jacket pocket flaps is torn. I have to arrange the suits I brought with me in the walk-in, and place them next to the arrangement of Zach's clothes that I would never wear.

After I had discarded one suit for another, I went back to admire the bathroom once more. This body looked plenty respectable when I turned to the mirror this time, and I decided I should take it for a walk. I was coming down the stairs, on the verge of whistling a jaunty annoying tune for some reason, when the door at the base of the steps opened inward.

"Hi, honey," she said, her back to me as I descended the last few steps. "Did you take down the sign?"

I stopped at the landing, let this body's eyes flash as she turned.

"Yeah," I said. "I did."

She looked at me, cast a look around the living space, and backed up a step.

To her credit, she didn't scream.

VIII.

It all started rather well, and I had high hopes for the situation. My voice was calm and controlled when I spoke, and this body's eyes were locked on hers.

"Kendra," I said. "There have been some recent developments that you might want to consider from a slightly more expansive perspective than you may be used to."

She blinked, but she didn't look away.

"Where's Zach?" she said. "Who are you?"

I would have killed her right there, if she weren't so calm and pretty. I had imagined blonde hair and blue eyes when I heard her name, and I hadn't bothered to look closely at the pictures as I was throwing them out. Her eyes and hair were dark, and her olive skin was flawlessly compelling. Intelligence glinted in the almond shapes of the windows to her soul, and I found more behind those eyes than I had in her husband's. We were standing pretty close to each other, and she would have been more uncomfortable if I wasn't soothing her through that visual connection; still, there was a calm within her that I hadn't put there.

I moved closer, physically, deliberately.

"You know Zach isn't right for you, don't you?" I asked.

This body's voice was calm and measured, so it wasn't that causing the break in our connection. I had chosen the wrong words, stepping in too close and too fast, and now she was looking away. It was with great admiration that I watched her gather her wits about her, and bolt for the door. Even when I grabbed her, Kendra didn't scream. She fought me with more fervor than her guy had, but this body was stronger than ever. It wasn't long before I was draining another body into the tub, and looking for another inter-dimensional space to put it.

I had to remind myself the entire time that I was severely limited by my inherent lack of continuity. Taking on a human's deoxyribonucleic acid profile means taking on a bunch of other stuff with it, and leaving behind whatever it is I may have had before. The mere fact that I keep promising myself that I won't kill anyone else is evidence of my own higher nature, and higher calling. It may be relevant that the promise is always made while I dispose of another body, but not nearly as relevant as the promise itself. Some human philosophies propose that the desire to strike a blow is equivalent to actually striking the blow; I would turn that around. Should I strike a blow, and wish that I didn't have to as I did or shortly after, surely that is a sign of a progressing soul.

Perhaps it is as evil to think of striking the blow as it is to strike it; and perhaps it is less evil to strike the blow and not think of it. It surely serves this body to have my memories fade so quickly from its organic circuitry, as even one lifetime's memories can be enough to freeze a soul's progress in place. I wonder while I change my suit yet again if only the ringer can achieve true adult innocence, and marvel that it could happen immediately after what less advanced folks might call a murder.

After two physical altercations, not counting the driver from earlier, changing clothes doesn't really freshen this body up properly. Its face has a scratch on it, and that perfect hair from earlier is mussed and flattened in the most unattractive manner. A shower does this body good, and by the time I get suited up again I realize that it's feeling more than a little hunger. All of the ingredients in the cupboards look like they would take some real planning to pull together, and it strikes me that it would be much easier to order pizza.

While I wait, I roam the house looking for things that I might give away to the neighbors, to unclutter the space and make some new friends. With the new year on the way, and time to do my ringing, it will be nice to put together a proper life before I go to work tearing another down. It's a special treat when I discover the wine collection, and imagine the odds that a neighborhood full of parents will quickly take in the new guy who brings over a bottle of wine every time he stops by.

There's no scotch, which is fine for now. This is California, and there are as many perks to that as there are drawbacks. One of those perks is booze in grocery stores, and I saw one right around the corner on the ride here. I'll make a trip a little later, after I've stuffed this body with pizza and taken my first friendly walk through the neighborhood.

IX.

It was hard not to be a little perfunctory about the first few visits. I was zeroing in on a target, and the last thing I wanted to do was walk right up to the door I wanted most to walk right up to. Zach had been right about the excess of tiny crumb munchers that inhabited the neighborhood. Every family I met had at least as many minor members as it had adults, and some more than that.

I didn't kill the pizza guy, by the way. I didn't even really think about it until just now, and I want to make sure there is no mistake about it.

The wine was indeed a popular item, as these were parents we were talking about here. I managed to give away half a dozen bottles of the fermented grape juice before I finally stepped on the porch I had been eyeing the whole time. This body's finger trembled slightly in anticipation as it neared the lighted button that would ring the doorbell.

Dogs started barking at the sound, the happy noise accompanied shortly by nearing footfalls. I tried on my most friendly smile, and felt this body's face finally getting used to my expressions.

As soon as he opened the door, I knew it was him.

It wouldn't do for me to call immediate attention to the ringing; it's likely that he hasn't even noticed it yet, it's still so dull and distant. Instead, I extend this body's right hand and hold that smile in place.

"Hi there, neighbor," I said. "I just moved in a few houses down, and I wanted to stop by and introduce myself. My driver's license says Clyde Morgan, but you can call me Ring."

The door came open wider, and I could almost see the happiness in the air inside the house. He returned my smile, then the handshake.

"Hi, Ring," he said. "I'm Henry. Nice to meet you. We're wrapping up a delicious meal, and we're about to dig in to some homemade chocolate cake. Why don't you join us?"

I held out the bottle I had brought with me.

"Oh, no," I shook this body's head. "I don't want to impose. I just wanted to say hi, and bring you a bit of wine."

He took the bottle, held it up and turned it in the light.

"Sure you won't come in?" he asked. "Stephanie's going to want some of this, especially if you come in."

I shrugged.

"Well," I said, "if you're going to twist my arm..."

Henry laughed, and stepped aside. Everything hit me at once as I walked in, but I played it off like it was just the smells. I turned to face him as he shut the door, and sniffed dramatically at the air.

"Wow," I said. "Dinner was pretty epic, huh? Garlic and onions and some kind of fish that smells absolutely amazing. Is that salmon?"

Henry laughed.

"It was," he said. "Sorry, friend. You'll have to settle for a glass of wine and a slice of cake. Come in, meet my family."

That was the main part of what had washed over me,

not some dead cooked fish filet. Henry's family was all kind words and bright smiles, and his wife did want to try the wine right away. I pretended to enjoy the syrupy purply stuff, until Henry said he was going to join us in his own way. Soon I was watching him tilt a bottle with a black label that struck the most pleasant of chords in my memory, and she was watching me watch him with a happy twinkle in her eye.

"Ring?" she murmured.

"Yeah?" I said, distracted.

I turned this body's head, but I didn't make eye contact. I was still watching Henry, putting the cap back on and setting down the bottle, letting the first warm textured taste wash over his tongue and swirl around the back of his mouth. I knew the motion, subtle as it was from the outside.

"Ring." She was laughing now, between sips of wine.

"Yeah." I met her eyes, and raised one of this body's eyebrows.

"Would you rather have scotch?" She was still laughing.

I was a little flummoxed, more so when Henry stepped close again.

"Hey, Ring," he said, "I'm sorry. I figured you wanted wine, since you brought wine. You want some scotch? Or something else? We've got—"

"Scotch would be great," I said. "Maybe with an ice cube or two, if I could..."

Henry laughed, and Stephanie joined in once more. I had to fight to keep tears from this body's eyes, with the happy and good-natured joy I felt all around me. It was almost too much when the whisky hit this body's lips, but I managed to keep it together. With the taste still in my mouth, I glanced out into the expansive living area beyond the dining room. The kids were watching television, each of them laying cuddled with a dog that looked exactly as happy as the child petting on it.

I brought my attention back to the table, raised the glass.

"Well, it's official," I said. "You are the coolest family in the neighborhood."

They both smiled, and clinked their glasses against mine, and drank.

"Stephanie," I said. "There is a bunch of wine at my place, it came with the house. Why don't you two come by tomorrow, and you can pick out whatever you like?"

"Oh no, I couldn't..." She sipped the wine.

"It will only get given to less cool neighbors," I said.

Henry nudged her. "That would be a shame."

Stephanie sipped some more, considered it.

"We are pretty cool," she mused.

"Great," I said. "It's settled. Come by tomorrow, and I'll load you guys up."

I stood up, after I finished the scotch. They exchanged a glance, and I pretended not to notice. Couples seem to think they're secretly communicating with each other sometimes, when all too often they're really broadcasting everything to the world. They nodded in turn, decision made.

"Will you come for dinner after?" Stephanie asked. "It's the only way we'll feel okay about taking all your wine. And make no mistake, we will be taking all of your wine."

<h1 style="text-align:center">X.</h1>

It was less than a mile to the grocery store, and I didn't need much. Both of the cars in the garage would seem suspicious were I to use them, so I thought it best to walk. Even in early December, the weather was more warm than chilly. There were only a few sections of the market for me to hit up, and I thought it would be an in and out kind of scenario.

After the cans of soup, I hit the freezers. There was no need to feed this body with top shelf stuff, and food has never appealed to me in and of itself. A half dozen frozen dinners made it into the little basket I was carrying, and when I turned to find the booze I nearly bumped into someone.

That's the weird thing, in this situation or others like it. You don't sneak up on a ringer, no matter how good you are at sneaking. Fish have organic motion detectors that run the entire length of their bodies, and ringers have something completely different that functions in much the same way. Call it soul resonance or energetic sensitivity or whatever you like, there is no way that I could think I was alone in an aisle when there was a mortal right there with me.

"Hi," she said, eyeballing the frozen fake meat. "Don't I know you?"

At that point I would have cracked wise, ordinarily. A ringer can only be mistaken for someone other than they are, and it happens often enough that we get sick of hearing that type of question. The joke is always an inside one, but there is only a small percentage of a ringer's conversations that we don't have internally. I was thrown off by being thrown off, and more thrown off by knowing it should not have been possible for me to be thrown off in the first place.

It was all very disconcerting.

The fact that she was beautiful had nothing to do with it. I mumbled something about being new to the neighborhood, trying to get my breathing under control while not fumbling with my assortment of dinner choices. I saw her eyeball the collection of frozen preservatives, and shake her head.

"No," she said, "I haven't seen you around here. It was at the airport, maybe. Or on a flight. Do you remember something about a flight?"

Before the disconcerting feeling could wear off, I felt myself moving right into confused panic. The way she phrased that question was only the first part of it; the fact that it did spark a memory added fuel to the fire, and the trailing mist that the memory became as I reached for it turned the blaze to wildfire. This body wouldn't breathe right, no matter how I coached it, and I was starting to feel sweat beading up on its brow.

It's always amusing to use the word 'coincidence', for me. Those of us that move deliberately within the system don't necessarily know exactly how it works, but we do know more about it than those moving through life without really understanding what it is they're moving through. When the universe brings two people together, it is never by chance. That's just not how the system works. I explain this to clear up why I would thank the system for its timely and interlinked nature at this point, and that I only use the word 'coincidence' to poke fun at anyone who might make their way through life mistakenly thinking it is actually full of somehow accidental encounters.

"Ring!" It was another female voice, one I consciously recognized. I turned to the sound, felt my breath come back to me.

"Stephanie!" I sound way too excited, but she did save me.

As she approaches, I notice that the other woman is watching her carefully. I narrow this body's eyes, to size up why she would be sizing her up. Stephanie is no dummy, and she sees it too; her natural reaction is to smile and extend her hand in the most friendly manner.

"Making new friends already?" Stephanie asks.

She moves in, forcing the other woman to clasp her hand in friendship or risk being rude in the grocery store. The woman clasps Stephanie's hand.

"I'm Stephanie," she says, pumping the woman's hand. "My husband and I shared a bottle of wine with Ring last night. He's our new favorite neighbor. What's your name?"

It all comes out so fast and smooth, I nearly miss the slight inflection Stephanie puts on certain words. Like husband. I start to rush in, to correct her and steer her away from orchestrating some extra time between this body and this woman that makes it so uncomfortable to inhabit. It's too late.

"I'm Cassandra," the woman says. "Nice to meet you, Stephanie."

At the sound of her name, another thread of memory starts to unravel in this body's brain. She said it all slow and careful, like she knew it would have some effect. I try to play it off, and make a big show of looking completely disinterested in the exchange. It seems to annoy Cassandra, and befuddle Stephanie, so I keep it up.

After they've exchanged polite goodbyes, I find myself alone in the frozen section with someone that doesn't impair my ability to make this body breathe at all.

"Thanks," I say.

I stick this body's face in the cool freezer for a few seconds, peering at a few things but not reaching in for any of them. I close the glass door, and turn to Stephanie with a smile.

"I thought I'd never get away from that one," I say.

I let her have one last good look at the sad assortment of meal options I'm carrying around, and tell her I'll see her tonight. Then I get some scotch, and hurry it on back to the house.

XI.

There's some kind of song that keeps playing in the distance, quiet enough that I suspect it of being carved into the grooves of this body's brain. It's only slightly less annoying than the realization that I don't have a clean suit for tonight, and it gets forgotten as it drifts away. I have to rifle through clothes that I wouldn't be caught ringing in to find something that might work, and the earworm comes back while I do.

It's all too much, and I am in khakis and a sweater that could effectively be marketed as birth control when the doorbell rings. I can't help but savor the sound, and let this body's eyes roll back in its head in momentary madness or bliss.

I remembered what the sound indicated then, and rushed down the stairs. Still wearing the khakis and the orangish libido-killer, of course. When I opened the door, I did my best to hide my excitement at seeing them. I ushered them inside, apologizing for my inability to get some decent clothes shipped from my old place, and led them to the bottles that lined one wall.

"This is way more Stephanie's thing," Henry said, by way of apology. "I don't mean to be ungrateful, or disinterested. I only get into wine when we go out to wineries, that's all. I'm more about the people and the ambiance than the wine."

"Well, then," I felt the smile on this body's lips, "it's a good thing I got some scotch as well. I've got a bottle for tonight, and another that I opened as soon as I got home from the store. Let's have a sip, while she picks out what she wants."

Stephanie straightened from her bent position, and shook her head.

"I was kidding last night," she said. "I'm not now. I want it all. Especially this entire section of California Pinot Noir. Are you sure you don't want this wine, Ring? It's good stuff."

I shrugged.

"I want to make friends with my new favorite neighbors," I said, marveling at the way honesty felt. "I do have an ulterior motive."

She laughed, and nudged Henry.

"I saw him today at the store," she said.

"Yeah?" Henry raised an eyebrow.

"Yeah," she echoed. "He was buying a bunch of frozen crap. I don't think we should let him eat any of it. Let's take all his wine, and make him come eat real food with us until he gets settled in."

"Uh, guys," I said. "I'm right here."

They laughed, and Henry turned slightly away from me to form a conspiratorial circle of mock secrecy.

"Stephanie," he said. "I think we should start hanging out with this guy. We've been talking about not having any adult friends, and everyone else in the neighborhood is so boring. Sweater and khakis aside, he seems like a pretty okay guy."

Stephanie glanced my way, raised an eyebrow, and ducked back into their huddle.

"He said he has better clothes on the way," she remarked. "It's really the only thing off about him."

"They're not even mine," I protested, which earned me a mock dirty look from both of them. Still, I felt the need to explain. "The previous owner left them behind. It's all I had, really."

It was adorable, them sharing a bemused look and then glancing at me suspiciously, only to turn and share another critical telepathic exchange. They nodded together, finally, and turned to me as one.

"Other people's clothes aside," Henry said, smirking, "we think we want you to be our new friend. Dinner is at six sharp every night, and there will be consequences for tardiness or unexcused absences. Do you accept the terms of our proffered friendship?"

I was as serious about this as they were being silly about it, and I made sure my grin wasn't a ghastly one.

"We better grab some wine and scotch, then," I said. "It's going to be dinner time soon, and I don't want to be late. Let's get going."

While we gathered bottles, I felt obliged to make an observation.

"You guys are weird," I said, smiling. "Thank the system."

Henry stopped gathering, and looked at me.

"Did you say 'thank the system?'" he asked.

I thought back, nodded.

"Like a normal person might say 'thank God'?" he pressed me.

I shrugged.

"Well, yeah," I said. "I guess so. That's ignorant, though. Most of the people that say that don't refer to a deity when they do; they are speaking of the only thing that is all things, of the thing their book calls omnipotent and omnipresent. If it is all things, it is not somewhere within the system; it is the system itself. Even the most powerful god exists within some kind of framework, and is thus limited in both power and presence. The system is the framework. All mortal and immortal activity happens within it."

Henry gave me a really funny look then, and surprised me with how serious his face got suddenly.

"Ring," he said. "Do you think about that sort of thing a lot?"

Stephanie had an expression of earnestness on her face that I couldn't miss, and I read the situation pretty clearly in the space of time it took for this body to draw a careful breath.

"Sure," I said, with another shrug. "I prefer to have a little scotch in me when I do, the way the system intends it, but I think about why and how we are here doing this whole life thing on a pretty regular basis."

They exchanged another look, and I thought for a moment that she was going to hug one of us. Then Henry smiled, and elbowed me.

"Now who's the weird one?" he said.

XII.

There wouldn't be any memories of sitting down and eating dinner with a normal family like a normal person in this body's memory banks, even if it were focused on saving them. I was pretty sure about that, although it felt like such a natural and comfortable thing to do. Rather than observe the event from my usual perspective of aloof criticism, I found this body fully engaged in the complexity of simplicity.

Names have always been a little tricky for me. As someone who knows no reality other than one of switching bodies like others might change their outfit, names have a little trouble meaning as much to me as they do to folks that see their body as their own. It was the only aspect of the dinner experience that I practiced deliberately. As normal as the whole thing may have seemed to the rest of them, I was making a considerable effort to both relax and pay close attention.

I listened, when they asked the kids about their day at school. The boy was all excitement and playground stories, and I repeated his name in my head while he told them. After he had regaled us with a tale that no one over ten years old could follow, or even find the least bit interesting, I spoke it aloud to further cement the knowledge.

"Wow, Dylan," I said. "That's some pretty serious adventuring. It sounds like your high school is a lot more fun than mine was."

"He's not in high school," the other miniature human piped up. "He's in second grade."

Stephanie smiled at me across the table, and shook her head.

"He knows that, sweetie," she said. "He's playing."

"Yeah, Emily," her brother piped up. "Even I knew that."

Emily, I thought. *Emily, Emily, Emily.*

"Yeah, Emily," I said, echoing Dylan and my thought. "I know you're older than him. That's why you have your driver's license, and he doesn't. You don't have to tease the poor kid, just because he isn't looking for a job yet. That kind of stuff is for young adults, like you."

She was not as amused by my playfulness as her brother, and she shot each of her parents an exasperated look before she turned it on me.

"I'm eight," she said. "I don't have a driver's license."

The boy was studying me across the table, in earnest.

"Mister Ring," he said. "How old are you?"

I laughed. "Well," I said, "my identification says one thing, but my memories say quite another. Of all the parts of me there are, not one of them feels the age that I am obliged to tell people when they ask that question. Even science is starting to tell us that our bodies replace themselves gradually over time, so it makes sense that most of us would feel much younger or much older than we actually do. Personally, I like to think I've been around since the beginning in one form or another."

I shrugged, and poked at a piece of the home cooked meat on my plate. Before I put it in this body's mouth, I smiled at the boy and added one last thing.

"And call me Ring," I said.

Now Henry was watching me, and obviously enjoying the way I was enjoying his family and fare. After I complimented Stephanie's cooking for the third or fourth time, he asked me about that.

"Why Ring?" he said. "That's not at all like your name. How did you pick up a nickname like Ring?"

I felt this body smiling, as I formulated an answer.

"Have you ever heard of resonant inductive coupling?" I asked.

Rather than wait for a response, I went on.

"Energy can be transferred through sound frequency," I said. "My line of work is driven largely by the evolution of power sources in organic reconstruction. The most amazing transfers are often done without wires or fibrous connections, and those transfers cause a unique ringing sound."

The whole family was watching me curiously, except Henry. He had a look of doubt on his face that made me wish I had let him answer my rhetorical question before stringing together a bunch of words off the cuff.

"I have heard of resonant inductive coupling," he said. "I don't think it works quite that way, Ring."

I waved my hand, and laughed.

"It sounded good, though," I came back. "Am I right?"

Henry relaxed a little, and I leaned into it.

"Actually," I said, "you got me. I know very little about the technology involved. I'm mostly sales, which means I ring a lot of doorbells. Maybe that's why they call me Ring. I'm more accustomed to simple exchanges, and I usually have spec sheets for the scientific stuff. I guess that means you're more techie than I am, Henry. What do you do?"

It only took a quick glance at each of them to see it wasn't the way to go. Henry suddenly looked more lifeless than I had ever seen him, and Stephanie let her eyes glass over in complete disinterest.

"I'm a software engineer," he said. "I'm totally grateful for my job, and the life it affords us. But I leave my work at work."

Stephanie nodded, and got up to start clearing the empty plates. I checked my watch, making a show of the motion, and stood as well.

"Well, thanks," I said. "That was a great dinner."

Henry remained seated.

"You're not leaving, are you?" he asked. "Didn't you bring a black box with you? You'll drink wine with my wife, but you won't stay and have a glass of scotch after dinner like a gentleman?"

I sat down again, let my smile show.

XIII.

I let this body's eyes roam the perfect space. It was like a man cave that had been created on set, for some television show, with nothing spared but the actual amount of square footage it took up.

"Hey, Henry," I said, holding up my glass. "Cheers."

Taking in the room with another sweeping glance, I nodded my approval. It was not the secret shop of yesteryear, with organized messes on every surface and pictures of naked ladies on the walls. The furniture was sparse and tasteful, barstools around the bar and easy chairs around the flatscreen. Actual art hung on the walls, beautiful landscape portraits speaking of faraway lands with a voice anyone with eyes could hear. The bar had a single tap, and the handle was a familiar orange face, with mohawk and sunglasses and all.

"Is this where we smoke?" I quipped.

"Yeah." Henry nodded. "I'll turn on the air purifier."

I waved him back to his easy chair, laughing.

"Just kidding," I said. "This is such a reversal of the area a man usually inhabits in his home. It's like you're not hiding anything in the toolbox or the tackle box."

Henry looked confused.

"There's no toolbox in here," he said. "No tackle box

either. I don't fish, Ring. And I don't have anything to hide. Not from my wife, anyhow."

I nodded. "Exactly."

I took another sip of the liquid magic with the black label.

"Unlike you," Henry added.

This body's throat constricted around the last of the drink, and I coughed as I tried to take it into its lungs instead. Setting down the glass, I made a big show of clearing my throat. When I was finished, Henry was still studying me closely.

"You're not a salesman, Ring," he said. "You're a top aide to a senator, or you were until yesterday. That's when you went missing, along with your security detail."

I laughed again, picked up the glass.

"Some security detail," I said. "It was one guy."

Henry frowned.

"One guy who still hasn't shown," he said. "Not only that, you are wanted for questioning about the bodies found at the airport."

It should have been a lot more awkward, him leveling these things at me far from any easy exit. I knew why I wasn't worried; it was a curious thing, that Henry wasn't.

"I hadn't heard about that," I said, offhandedly. "Which airport?"

He was still frowning.

"It's Sacramento," he said. "There's only one."

"Of course," I nodded. "Who were they?"

There was only so much I could do, to string him along enough to tune into why Henry wasn't concerned to be in a room with what he thought might be a killer. If it went too far, things might take a turn that I didn't want them to take. It was earlier than I generally like to do it, but it seemed a good time for the reveal. Henry was looking at me like he was questioning his decision to feel safe with me, and I couldn't have that.

"Alright," I said. "I'll tell you."

He cocked an eyebrow at me, and reached for the bottle I had brought with me. I was glad to see my glass go from dreadfully empty to comfortably full in one friendly lean, and the warm cool taste on this body's tongue got me talking.

"The fabric of the universe is a strange thing," I began. "It seems solid and stronger than steel in so many ways, yet it's a gossamer web that trembles at every thought we think within it. Do you know that everything flashes in and out of existence at the alarming rate of a bunch of times per second, and the only thing that makes us see it as solid and sustaining is the way in which we perceive it? Like a film flashing across a lighted lens, the illusion of continuity in our lives is akin to the illusion of movement in a movie."

Damn this body, and its love of movies.

"What?" Henry said.

"What makes it go away?" I finished for him. "What makes it come back? How do we know if we existed a moment ago, or if we will exist a moment from now? Only the system can know, and it's not fond of revealing such secrets."

There was a pretty long silence then, in which I noticed that Henry had drained his drink while I was talking. It seemed only polite that I should do the same, and soon he was filling our glasses again. Either he had great timing, or mine was getting a little off. When he spoke again, I found myself choking once more on whisky that tried to go down the wrong way.

"I'm dying, then," he said.

It was a simple sentence, spoken with such casual ease that my coughing fit seemed like a disproportionately dramatic reaction. I couldn't help it this time, and I went back over the words I had chosen to see how I had managed to give it away so soon. There had been a real and true vagueness to my message, and I wan't planning on dropping that bomb on him until the scotch was a little closer to gone.

After this body got its breath back, I tried to be reassuring.

"I wouldn't put it that way, necessarily," I said. "There's a big change coming in your life, and I'm here to help you through it. Did you lament puberty when it came your way? Do you resist the renewal of your body's cells, or the way it discards the old? When your body sprouted hair in strange places and filled your mind with new thoughts and desires, did you have a funeral for the child you no longer were? Did you change your body's birthday, or its name, when it changed its appearance?"

Henry didn't look terribly impressed or soothed by my words.

"Maybe you should go now," he said, quietly.

XIV.

"Everything within the system," I pressed on, "is both constantly dying and continually being born. It's a rare occasion when someone is there to assist with a difficult transition."

Henry looked at me, then his drink, and back at me.

"Thanks," he said. "I'm dying, but I've got a friend to help me through it? What exactly is your role in all of this, Ring?"

I sighed. "You're the one that keeps saying that, not me."

"What?" He frowned. "That I'm dying? Tell me I'm wrong. Tell me I'll be the same soul in the same body for years to come, and that I'm wrong about what you're trying to say."

It seemed a good time to shrug.

"Henry," I said. "I couldn't honestly say that to anyone. Like I've been saying, the nature of life is far too transitory for a statement like that to ever be true. For you, or anybody else."

He laughed, and it was the first real spark of anger I had seen in him. There was no humor to the sound, only exasperated frustration.

"Without riddles," he snapped. "Tell me I'm wrong, or tell me I'm right. Stop with the vague platitudes already."

I nodded.

"Alright, then," I said. "You're dying. Feel better?"

His anger was diffused instantly, and Henry leaned back into the comfort of his recliner. Swirling the remaining whisky around in his glass, he nodded quietly to himself. I let him be as alone with his thoughts as he could be with me in the room. Obviously, he needed to be the one driving this train. As accustomed as I was to leading souls to the other side in my own way, I got that he would feel better about all of this if he felt like he was somewhat in control.

It didn't help that everything I discovered about the way his mind worked made me more fond of him, when I thought of the end.

"It's funny," Henry said. "I felt like I was desperately running for so long, putting everything into place. All through school I worked, and saved. As soon as I graduated, I worked twice as much. By the time I met Stephanie, I was in a great place in my career. It's a good thing, too. She became my everything right away, in the strangest way."

He glanced at me, and I nodded for him to go on.

"It was different than anything I ever felt," he continued. "It was like making her happy made me happy, and right away I couldn't imagine life without her. I took her house hunting after we had been dating a couple of months, and proposed to her while we were looking at this house. It was the same as it had been with her, I knew it was right. Within a week we were moving in, and I felt like I could really get started taking care of her the way I wanted to. It was the same with the kids, too. Every part of my life that has come from being with her felt like something I wanted to do so badly that it would pain me not to do it. It's where all my joy comes from, and I have a lot of joy. But that's not all."

I was spending a lot of time looking around, and visually inspecting the contents of my glass. Only when I felt he needed it did I look Henry's way, or when I wanted him to keep talking. I looked at him now, raised one of this body's eyebrows to indicate the interest I truly felt.

"The whole time," Henry said, "I felt like I was rushing toward one thing after another, trying to get all of the pieces in place before the board got yanked from under me and the game ended. I needed to be a good husband, for her and for me. I needed to know that she knew she was loved, even adored, and that nothing could take that experience from her. Same with the kids, I needed them to know I loved them so much that I wouldn't do anything but work and hang out with my family for the longest time."

Henry had a good look around the space we were occupying, indicated the setting with a nod and a smile.

"Stephanie insisted I build this," he said. "We didn't need a three car garage, and the space was only getting neglected. She told me I should wall it off, and make a man cave. She said that it would make her and the kids happiest if they knew I was doing something to make myself happy, so I did it. I mostly come out here and watch the news, since she hates that stuff. And I drink, and think. Sometimes I'll smoke a cigar, which seems to help with both the thinking and the drinking."

Henry emptied the bottle, between our glasses, and laughed.

"I don't usually drink this much, though," he mused.

I shrugged.

"Call me a bad influence, then," I said.

The way he shook his head was a pretty good indicator of how well the drink had saturated his thinking. I felt like I knew him better than I should have by now, had time spent together been the only source of information available to me. Henry didn't strike me as being prone to dramatic gestures, or exaggerated head movements.

"No, Ring," he said.

There was a touch of a slur there, and he noticed as surely as I did.

"No," he said again, clearly. "This is the first time in my life that everything has made sense. I actually don't spend as much time watching the news as I lead most people to believe. I mean, I keep up on things. I know you're not who you appear to be. But that's not all I do out here. I've taken to reading books, the kind of books that people like me don't normally read. I've been kind of expecting you, for a while."

XV.

This body's head was swimming with the same sweet intoxication that was lighting Henry's eyes. I kept drinking, that I might swim more deeply in it, and let a question roll off my tongue. Something was thick in this body's mouth, either the question or its tongue, and my words came out more slurred than his had.

"Just who do you think I am?" I asked.

Well, I asked something like that. Turn all the 'tee' sounds to 'ess' sounds in that sentence, and you get a better idea of the actual noise that issued forth from this body's mouth.

"I don't know," he said. "If I had to guess..."

I nodded for him to go on, and guess, since his words were so much more clearly enunciated than mine. This body had nearly altogether forgotten how to breathe.

"I'd say you're some kind of walk-in," he said. "Your soul or spirit or essence stepped into someone else's body, probably to stop him from killing more people. Am I anywhere close to right?"

I nodded again, and contemplated the liquid still swirling in my glass. It took a few seconds of deliberate thought and breathing to formulate and deliver a coherent answer, and he was kind enough to wait.

"I like that term," I said. "Walk-in. That's not what I call myself, but it's a somewhat accurate description of what I do. I did shift this body's energy, and change the direction its life was headed in. It didn't have to do with him hurting others, as much as it had to do with soul continuity and systemic interdependence. Sometimes I ring in folks like him, and sometimes I ring in guys like you. It's got little to do with how good or evil a person's day to day life appears to be going on the surface. Someone once said that the entire universe would collapse for want of a single atom, and they were right on more than one level. Butterfly wings are not just a factor in time, they play an equally important role in space. What you do affects me, and everyone and everything else within the system. If the proverbial butterfly flaps its wings in the wrong place at the wrong time, the whole thing goes poof."

"Poof?" Henry elevated an eyebrow. "Really, Ring? Poof?"

I shrugged, and swilled back the rest of my drink.

"The end is far less likely to be a dramatic explosion that everyone hears than a quiet winking out of existence that no one notices," I said.

He finished his drink too.

"You're a pretty dark guy," he said. "I mean, for an elevated soul that walked into someone else's life to right all the wrongs he may have committed or may be about to commit."

I stood up, wavered in place while I came back.

"I never said I was elevated," I said, although I didn't necessarily disagree with the assessment. "And right and wrong are not nearly as fixed from the systems's perspective as they are from most people's. There's order in the universe, obviously, but it isn't based on any individual's perception of good or evil. I mean, that would imply that the system itself is fundamentally flawed."

Under normal circumstances, I wouldn't have pointed it out so soon. With all the scotch swimming around in this body's belly, it seemed a good idea at the time. I leaned forward, squinting so there was only one Henry, and flicked him lightly on the forehead with a middle finger. For a moment I thought I had missed, as he looked at me in befuddled curiosity; then his eyes went wide with wonder, and Henry forgot I was even in the room.

I let him come to grips with his expanded reality, standing there and waiting patiently if not too steadily. It was a good opportunity to work on my breathing, and reestablish some semblance of equilibrium. After a few minutes his eyes came back into focus, and found me watching him.

"What was that?" he breathed. "How did you...?"

He swirled his hand through the air, tracking it visually like it was trailing magic sparks.

I laughed.

"That should have put it in perspective," I said. "I just gave you a little bit more soul awareness than you're accustomed to. Spend some time with that, and get in touch with the experience of continuity that it provides. It should have sobered you up some, too. You really shouldn't be drinking so much on a school night, Henry."

As an afterthought, I waved my hand mysteriously between us.

"That will help, too," I said, although I hadn't done anything. "You won't be hung over in the morning."

Henry laughed, the joyous boyhood sound of a man letting go.

"I never get hangovers," he said.

I moved toward the door, nodding wisely and bumping the coffee table twice as I did.

"See?" I said. "I am wise beyond my years."

Henry swept past me, opened the door into the rest of the garage.

"I thought you said you've been around since the beginning," he said, as he passed me. "How wise can a body be?"

"Ah!" I bumped into the doorjamb, and turned slightly to lean on it.

"I'm not a body, though," I said. "I'm certainly not this body. My consciousness is filtered through it, but it is neither fully expressed nor completely contained by it. I'm wiser than a body can be, because I'm not a body. I'm a ringer."

He led me through the house, since I kept losing my way. It was suddenly of great concern to me, that Henry sleep well on his new knowledge tonight.

"Did I explain well enough?" I said. "Are you okay to sit with this new reality by yourself? Do you understand that you can't talk to anyone about this?"

We were on the porch when he answered, and he kept his voice down for everyone's sake.

"That thing you did," he said. "That helped a lot. Your explanation of who you are and what you do was about as circuitous and convoluted as your version of resonant inductive coupling, but that helped a lot."

I stood there, smiling, until he realized what I was waiting for.

"That way," he said, pointing. "That house right there. That's yours. Can you make it, buddy?"

I nodded my thanks, and headed off in that general direction.

XVI.

There was no good reason for me to be waking up on the couch, with two perfectly comfortable beds in the house. That's where I found myself late the next morning, with this body still swathed in the worst possible collection of fabrics and its head throbbing like it wanted to break open. It took a full five minutes of breathing to collect my thoughts, and the sweater still made this body's stomach twist as I glimpsed it in the mirror. Right in the middle of transforming my breathing from burnt scotch to minty fresh, I had to turn and lurch for the toilet.

Most of the vomit made it in the bowl, and as the sound of swirling water died away that tune twisted through this body's brain again. Cursing and brushing teeth turned out to be mutually exclusive, so I opted for the fresh breath. The only thing a shower had to offer was a fresh outpouring of last night's intake, and whisky sweat soaked the jeans and concert tee I donned before I was out the door.

There's a jug of spackling paste in the hallway, and I trip on it in my haste to get out the door. It strikes me as strange, and more so since I don't remember it having been there before; so I take it into the garage and place it by one of the cars. It's in this flummoxed state that I step outside, searching for the key that will lock the door while I'm out.

"Excuse me."

I jump at the voice behind me, but somehow this body doesn't. I'm glad for it, and I turn to smile at whoever is standing on my porch.

"Sorry," I say, still flummoxed. "I'm not interested."

He's still standing there when I find the key, and slide it into the lock. For some reason, he's peering past me and through the open door.

"Where's Zach?" he says, all huffy.

Leaning away from what I'm doing, I give him a clear look at the action my hand is taking. There's no reason to obstruct the view he already had, or slam the door on both of us.

"Zach moved," I said. "Did you not know they were selling the house? The sign was on the lawn, right over there."

I pointed, smiled in the most friendly fashion.

"It's gone, now," I said. "Because I bought the place. That means they left, and I live here now."

He wasn't the kind of face you might see smiling at you from the cover of a magazine or anything; but when he narrowed his eyes, he turned into a downright ugly person.

"I know they're selling," he said. "They were still here two days ago. Now Zach isn't answering his phone, and you're living in his house."

There's a certain kind of energy that radiates off a fellow that has a desire to get violent. This guy was definitely radiating, and I was starting to feel a little radiant myself.

"Listen, brainy," I say, letting my smile evaporate, "it sounds like Zach was as eager to end your friendship as he was to sell his house. You might want to consider the possibility that you aren't exactly the ray of sunshine that you seem to see yourself as, and find someone with an appropriately dark and self-absorbed energy to hang out with. Zach wasn't really your type, and I can see why he isn't taking your calls."

I had called a cab, and it showed up at this point, so I started to pull the door shut. The guy got right up in my face, and angled himself so he was a half step into the house. I'd have to close the door on his foot, if I was going to.

"Why is their stuff still here?" he demanded. "Why are you wearing his shirt?"

His angry eyes went from me to the contents of my house, and back to me again. I shrugged.

"I bought it all, except the shirt," I said. "This is mine, despite your inability to wrap your head around the fact that Cheap Trick might have printed more than one of them. They wanted a fresh start, like I said. I've lived on the road for the last few years, and didn't want to go to the trouble of furnishing the place, so I offered them more for everything. They took it, and here we are. With you trespassing. Please, by all means, get off my property."

There may have been an expletive in that sentence, or maybe even two, but that's not how I remember it. The next thing I knew he was standing on the sidewalk in front of my house, fiddling with his phone; and I was off to get some clothes that didn't make me look like I was friends with a guy like that.

XVII.

It was nice to have a suit, and another bottle of scotch. It didn't hurt that I had brought cigars, either.

Henry was enjoying the smoke as thoroughly as he was the drink, and I was thoroughly enjoying getting to know him through his new expanded perspective.

"That thing you did, last night," he said.

I reached back through the tenuous fog of drink and memory, and looked at him with genuine curiosity.

"When you touched my forehead," Henry prompted. "Was that...did you open my third eye?"

I burst out laughing.

"No one who understands the spiritual perspective calls it that," I said. "Keep saying it that way, and it's sure to slam shut on you. You know that if you go blind in one eye, you lose very little vision. Right?"

"Yeah, sure," he said. "Having two eyes is more about depth perception than it is about expanding your field of vision. Without a second eye, it's difficult to tell how far away things are."

Nodding wisely, I put on my sage face and blew out a stream of cigar smoke.

"It's much the same," I said. "You have a spiritual perspective that adds another element to what you see, in that it brings it into context. If it were closed entirely, you couldn't remember your wife's name. If it were opened completely, the knowledge wouldn't matter."

Henry looked wiser than before, and I couldn't tell if it was his aura or if it was just the haze of cigar smoke between us. Maybe it was the way he held the smoking stub.

"That sounds like a third eye to me," he pointed out.

"Yeah," I said. "From a very limited perspective, where one is drawing from the scant memories of one human lifetime and disregarding everything else. That probably is what it sounds like. Flip that perspective around, however, and see things from the point of view of the light rather than the shadow it is casting. It doesn't look like an eye at all, then. It looks like a river of energy that connects us to our true self. Or a trickle, in most cases. Either way, there is no shutting or opening a river. It flows, regardless of whether or not the flow is acknowledged. Without that flow, there is no reason to create the first two eyes. They see nothing without it, as there is nothing there to see."

Henry nodded.

"I do feel more connected," he said.

"Right," I smiled. "Exactly right. You feel more connected. That doesn't mean that you are more connected, it means that you are now more aware of that connection. If you hadn't been connected before, you would not have existed. Your spiritual energy is not an expression of your body; it's quite the opposite. Your body is an expression of spiritual energy. Take away the body, and you will see that spiritual energy find another place to go. Take away the spirit, and you take away the context in which the body lives."

Shaking his head, Henry raised an eyebrow in consternation.

"This is the problem I have with those books I've been reading," he said. "They seem so unapologetically full of riddles, and one sentence seems to contradict the next all too often."

I shrugged.

"Were you to try to explain life to me," I said, "without starting at the beginning, it may seem like a much simpler explanation. It wouldn't make sense, however, no matter how easy it was to grasp. At least not to me."

Holding his cigar out in front of him, Henry eyed the thick tendril of smoke rising off the hot tip.

"Is there a way you can explain that?" he ventured. "How do we start at the beginning, when our awareness begins mid-game?"

"You can start by considering that possibility," I said. "And come up with an analogy that makes sense from where you are now."

His rolling chuckle lifted the corners of this body's lips with the curl of my own smile.

"I suppose you have one in mind," Henry said.

"As a matter of fact," I nodded. "I do."

I took another puff off the stogie, and a pleasured sip.

"Imagine, if you would," I said. "That long after people had gone extinct, an intelligent being came to Earth and found a car rotting in a field. Would they see that it was once a mode of transportation, that this knob was once the windshield wiper controller for glass that is long gone? That the rusted circle used to be a steering wheel? Or would they see it for what it has become, a glorified planter box? Without the original idea, and an understanding of what that original idea was, it's hard to fully understand a situation. Or a body, even one you call your own."

It was nice to sit in silence for awhile, and know my companion was feeling just as in touch with his soul as I was with mine for once.

"You spiritual types," he said, breaking it. "Aren't you supposed to be pretty holy? What's with the drinking? And the smoking? Aren't you supposed to be above that kind of thing."

I nearly spilled some of the scotch, I got so animated then.

"Listen, man," I huffed. "The most annoying thing about people that don't get it is the judgement they try to lay on those of us that do. Do you think this cigar somehow exists outside the system? Or aged scotch? The only thing we do by turning our backs on possibilities is turn our backs on possibilities. If the system didn't want me to drink and smoke, it wouldn't have made these things so delightful to partake in."

There was no ensuing silence; Henry came right back at me.

"Ring," he said. "The way you talk makes me wonder if maybe it wasn't you that killed those people. Also, it makes me wonder if maybe you're totally full of it. No offense."

"None taken." I drained my drink. "I was wondering when you'd figure it out. Not the killing thing; the other."

XVIII.

Apparently my new routine had become waking up in the morning and breathing my way to the other side of a hangover. The entire time I was lying down, I could feel the ache in this body's head. As soon as I breathed it into manageability, nature called rather urgently. While I padded to the bathroom, another surprise erupted. The last few steps down the hallway were made with a handful of vomit and a set of cheeks puffed tight with more of the nasty stuff.

Apparently my new routine needed some tweaking.

I had made it to the bedroom, at least. That meant my carpeted footsteps carved in partially digested goo could be closed up behind a door, and left for someone else to find. With my suits in another closet, I shifted my bathroom activities to the main washroom. It was bigger, and there was no reason for me to be running up and down stairs just to sleep and start my day. There was a bed down here, and more room to move about as I pleased.

Laying about seemed to be the best thing the day had to offer, and I got to it as soon as I had sweated out what I had taken in last night. I didn't want to shimmy into a suit, just yet, and found myself adequately satisfied with the sweats and logo shirt I found in a drawer.

There's something special about watching a movie, when you're a ringer. It's going to be the first time, in a way, no matter what. It's likely that it's not, though. That's when things get fun. Part of watching a movie that the body you're inhabiting has seen or that you've seen in another body is figuring out which it was. The other part is the fact that it really is like never seeing a single motion picture until you've become a fully formed adult. As much of the world as I've seen, and as long as I've been around, nothing tells a story like a movie. And nothing points out how movies are made a certain way, with certain assumptions in mind, than watching one for the first time through eyes that sparkle with spirit.

Not even ten minutes into the first story that the giant screen begins to weave, I feel the burrowing itch of an earworm. I pause the magic, and use up all the curse words I've got to get the blasted thing out of this body's mind. In the ensuing silence I wonder if this body is really the big movie fan, or if it might be me. Before I can consider, or put the story back in epic motion, the doorbell rings.

I'm not one to get upset at the sound of ringing, on a regular basis. The cursing that I choose to keep under my breath at this point is not due to the sound itself; that is sweet, and soothing on a soul level. My discontent is more a result of knowing that I am being summoned, and that there is no one in mind that I want to be summoned by right now. It might not be polite, but I let it boil to the point of rage by the time I fling open the front door.

It's as if I'm staring in a mirror that reflects only emotion. On one side of the threshold, I'm positioning this body in such a way as to clearly show that I left irritated behind long before opening the door. On the other side, standing on the porch, is the fellow that seems to think that his friend still lives here. He's got the same posture, the same rigid stance, and the same burning rage in his muddled eyes. The main differences evident are, of course, the faces we wear and the phone he is holding.

Without a word, he taps the screen with the hand not holding the device. Sound erupts behind me, the quiet earworm suddenly loud enough for me to pick out the lyrics. He holds the phone out, inches from this body's face, so I can read the screen.

'Calling Zach...'

I laugh, and don't mind that it sounds a little maniacal.

"Somebody was repairing dry wall in here," I muse, remembering. "It must have been Zach, and he must have dropped his phone in the wall before sealing it up."

Dude starts turning a little red, and I almost give him a quick lesson in angry breathing. Before I can, he points at the shirt that is covering this body's torso.

"That's his shirt!" He's squealing now, and getting loud. There hasn't been any eyes on us up to this point, a ringer can feel when they're being watched. With his elevated emotional state in mind, I look down at the logo on this body's chest.

It was all well and good when we were talking about Cheap Trick; there was no way I was owning up to the Powerpuff Girls.

"Aw, hell," I say, to indicate the gravity of the situation as it escalates. "You got me."

I reach out this body's arms, over the short distance he had left between us in his accusatory huff. They're batted away, just as I expected, and I let him charge into the hold he thinks he's got on me.

Slippery as a fish, I sidestep and let him launch himself awkwardly into the foyer. I close the door behind me, and lock the deadbolt.

XIX.

Draining his blood into the tub was not nearly as easy as the others had been. There was some real fight in that one, and I sensed that he would take his death better overall if he felt he had the upper hand for a little while. It turned out to be a terrible choice, like most kindness to strangers. By the time he gasped his last labored breath, there were smears of blood all over the once welcoming foyer.

It was kind of a shame, to lose the whole master suite and the front door all in such a short space of time. I comforted myself that both situations did not involve bodies, other than the one I was occupying. The other problem was the smell, which I first caught a whiff of when I sat down to finish the movie I had started. I started it over, and even made some popcorn; but I just wasn't in the mood for a story any more.

When I decided to go for a walk, I realized that Zach's buddy had parked his car in my driveway. I had to open the portal I had stashed him in once more, and fish his keys from his pocket. Another suit got stained, and another string of curses ensued when I saw that drifting apparition lingering at the entrance to the timeless space I had discovered. It looked skullish, and confused somehow, all at the same time.

I drove the car slightly further than I felt like walking, ditched it and got started. Every couple of blocks I ducked inside a business and browsed, so as not to stain this body's shirt with sweat. I found a nice sushi shop to eat some sticky rice and raw fish in, and a giant beverage store with a respectably long aisle of the spirit that is truly the most important. It was a couple bills for a couple of bottles, and I chose the one in blue. I didn't want to seem stuck on a theme, but I hate to fix things that are clearly not broken.

With the bottle in a bag, and a belly full of sustenance, the walk became more awkward as I got closer to home. I kept shifting the bagged bottle back and forth between this body's hands, and being keenly aware of how conscious I was of all the cars passing by. The fish kept shifting, with no prompting from me, and I felt the need to sit down for a spell. After only a few minutes, at the height of my discomfort, someone decided to occupy the bench beside me. I turned this body slightly away, to show my lack of desire for engagement, and she spoke anyhow.

"I get the feeling you don't like me," she said. "Why is that, Ring?"

Being so focused on getting this body's breath in proper order, it takes me a moment to decide if I want to transform the sounds she had made into words in this head. It takes another moment for the grudging transformation, and yet another for me to properly react.

I turn, and as soon as my eyes fall on her I lose complete track of this body's breathing. The first thought I have is to get up and run away, but that would look silly and childish. It's entirely possible that I've got her signals all wrong, and that she's coming at me from a completely different angle than the one I see her coming in from.

"Cassandra," I say, calm and at the first step of breathing right again.

I follow the word up with all the cleverness I can muster at this point.

"How are you." Stage two, breathing falling into a deep and natural rhythm. I didn't really ask a question, except in words; still she answers.

"I'm fine," she smiles. "It's you I'm concerned about."

Proper breath is a confidence builder, for sure. I can feel my own center coming into balance, and this body responding with clear thought and pleasant tingles. I'm neither purposefully paying attention to her nor deliberately ignoring her, and this is the worst possible place to try and figure out just what that angle I was wondering about before might be.

Now that I'm a little more firmly seated in this body, I'm becoming more aware of my surroundings and situation as well. I realize that I've parked it on a bench that is there for bus riders. Nodding at the sign, I speak without regard for what she had said.

"Which bus are you catching?" I say, keeping this body's eyes on the stack of numbers on the sign. None of it means anything to me.

"Twenty-one," she says. "At two twenty-nine, in about three minutes."

I nod, stand up and look down at her still sitting.

"Well, I'm walking," I said. "I'm sure that's all I need."

"Ring," she said. "Won't you sit with me, at least until the bus gets here? I don't think a brisk walk is going to solve everything, in this case."

I wave her off, while I walk away.

"Sorry, sister," I say, a little blithely.

When I reach the curb, I look back.

I'm not at all surprised that she isn't sitting there any more.

<h1 style="text-align:center">XX.</h1>

There's a car in the drive, when I return. I slow down as soon as I see it, and come very close to walking by my own house. The driver's door pops open as I approach, and I see Henry's head as he cranes his neck to holler out to me.

"Ring!" he says. "Hey, Ring!"

I feel the relief wash over me, and this body relaxes as I stop and make it smile.

"There he is," I say, like I was counting the moments until I saw him again. Since I kind of was.

He's out of the car by the time I get there, and we shake hands warmly. There's a part of him that is relieved to see me as well, and the contact lasts a little longer than it might ordinarily.

"Hey," I say, "shouldn't you be at work?"

Henry smiles, a little sheepishly.

"I couldn't keep my mind on what I was doing," he admits. "I took some sick leave, and spent most of the morning driving around. At some point I thought it would be nice to talk with you, if you had time. I've been sitting in your drive for an hour, thinking you were inside. No wonder you didn't notice me out here. Where were you?"

I shrug, hold out the paper bag. He takes it, and peeks inside. Henry's low whistle tells me he knows how much I spent for that single bottle, and he sounds impressed.

"Where did you get that?" he asks. "Not the grocery store."

He looks up and to the left, probably picturing a map of the nearby area. Shaking his head, he laughs.

"Did you seriously walk to BevMo?" he sniggers.

I shrug again, laugh with him.

"I went for a walk," I say. "I found a place to buy this sweet ambrosia along the way. Why are you questioning it? Let's go inside, drink some."

"Now?" He closes the car door. "It's barely three."

"Alright." I dig the keys from my pocket, and fit the right one into the deadbolt. "We'll go inside, and talk. You'll have to keep it light, though, if we aren't drinking. I don't have many rules, but the few I have are pretty hard and fast."

I throw open the door, and it hits us at the same time.

"Ring, what the..." he trails off. "What's that smell?"

It's hard to keep this body's nose from crinkling, and bile from rising in the back of its throat.

"Oh, yeah..." I frown, to keep from losing my fish. "I forgot. There's a bit of a mold issue with the house. I need to get a hotel, and have it fumigated."

Henry looks at me for so long that I start to think he wants me to be feeling uncomfortable.

"Ring," he says. "You don't need to lie to me. It's okay, I know you have a different life than..."

Trailing off, he looks at me in earnest. I can tell he's wrestling with how good he is, and my heart goes out to him. I let him finish, rather than complete his thought for him.

"...than anyone I know," he says. "You don't need to keep up appearances, if you don't want to. Come stay with us, and keep whatever money you have to treat yourself to what you can enjoy. I can't possibly understand what life is like from your perspective, but I get the sense that you haven't been able to let your guard down for awhile now. Get your things, and let's go home."

I laughed bitterly at the word. I didn't protest, though. As quick as I could, I went and got the suits and the cash. Before we got in the car, I showed him how much there was.

"I'd like scotch on the regular," I shrugged. "And a couple cigars a week, maybe. Otherwise, this is all for the party."

Henry knitted his brow. "Party?"

"Yeah," I said. "The New Year's Eve party."

He got all somber then, and I realized that he hadn't asked yet.

He did, now. "Will I be there?"

All the sudden I was patting his shoulder, trying to assuage the feelings that were inside this body somehow.

"Of course," I said. "It's going to be in your honor. That's the night, Henry. You have until the end of the year."

"Then poof?" He smiled, and I couldn't help but like him a smidgen more. "Alright. Let's have a party. What kind of event did you have in mind?"

I rubbed this body's hands together, curled its lips in an evil smile.

"A hall," I said. "With a full bar, and a bunch of drugs. Strippers, too. Lots of strippers. "

His look of discontentment was too much for me not to laugh.

"Holy system, Henry," I said. "I know you, dummy. Sort of. I thought it would be cool to invite your friends and family, and make sure you were able to spend a lot of time with your kids without it looking..."

It was my turn to trail off, and look away.

There was no bitterness to his laugh, and he was smiling for real when I got the nerve to look at him again.

"Without it looking like I know it's my last chance?" he said. "It's okay, Ring. Not many people get to have that. It's not a curse, not the way I see it. The way I see it, you're doing me a huge favor."

He thought about that, amended.

"More like," he said, "several big favors. It's why I want you to stay with us, and relax. You may be a bit of a shifty dude, but I sense that you have a really good heart under all your bluster and bull. I think you deserve a break, as much as someone like you can take one."

This body was getting all misty, and I frowned to keep its eyes dry. I got in the car, and kept my eyes looking out the window until Henry had started it up.

"One favor," he said, before we got going. "Don't kill anyone, while you're staying with us."

I nodded, solemnly, still looking out the window.

"Okay, Henry," I said. "I won't kill anyone while I'm staying with you and your family. Except you, of course. Sorry, buddy."

XXI.

It was over dinner that night, that Stephanie brought up the project Henry had only just gotten started on.

"Ring," she said, after I complimented her cooking for the hundredth time, "did Henry show you the plans he drew up for the mother-in-law unit he's building?"

I shook my head, chewed the savory sustenance for all the flavor it was worth. Henry wasn't drinking tonight, and neither was Stephanie. I didn't want to be the only one, at least until after dinner.

"No," I said, "In fact, I haven't even seen the back yard. How far along is it?"

It's different, talking to couples; questions are best put in a way that either of them can answer.

"Only barely," Henry answered. "We got it approved last week, and laid the foundation right away. Dylan did most of the work, so I know it's done well."

Emily chimed in, smirking.

"I supervised," she said. "Someone has to watch those two."

She exchanged a friendly but conspiratorial look with her mother.

"Well," I said, "if I'm staying with you guys, I should help out. Shall we get started after dinner?"

Henry waved off my urgency, glanced at the wall clock.

"Nah," he said. "It's getting dark too early. I'll grab what we need to get started on the way home from work tomorrow, and we'll get after it first thing on Saturday."

There were eyes on me, and I followed the feeling to Stephanie. She smiled, like she had been caught mid-mischief. This body's eyes narrowed playfully, and smiled back at her.

"What?" I asked her. "What's so funny?"

Stephanie's smile threatened to boil over into laughter. She gestured at my suit.

"You just don't seem like the handyman type of guy," she noted. "No offense, or anything. You're all about the suits and the scotch and the sales, right? When is the last time you swung a hammer?"

I shrugged, pushed some food around on my plate.

"My varied experience might just surprise you," I said. "Even if I can't remember most of it, I've done pretty much everything you can think of."

Now the eyes on me belonged to Henry, and I lifted this body's head enough to meet them across the table. He had a mildly terrified look on his face, as though he thought I was about to spill all my secrets.

"Besides," I added, "screws hold better than nails, and they're easier to remove. Unless Henry has a nail gun, I would think we'd be screwing this thing together."

Henry nodded, either in approval at the change of subject or in agreement.

"It will be nice to have the help," he said. "We only have a little while."

It was my turn to feel this body's eyes go wide, and train them on him. Maybe he did think the whole family needed to be in on the secret. I tried to think of something loud and pleasantly distracting to say, but none of the words in this body's brain wanted to find their way out of its mouth.

My internal panic was not lost on Henry, and he let me swirl about in it for a moment before he went on.

"The city gave us a deadline," he clarified, "like they do on all permitted builds. I don't think we need all the time they gave us, though. We should be able to get it finished by the end of the year."

While my breathing came back to me, I nodded in agreement and selected a forkful of deliciousness to bring to this body's mouth. Chewing it with the same care with which it had been prepared, I glanced at the kids in turn. After swallowing, and wiping this body's face with a napkin, I spoke in my usual calm manner.

"We can go over the plans," I said. "After dinner, instead of watching the news."

Stephanie nodded.

"Right?" she said. "Don't you hate the news?"

"Nah," I waved my fork. "Just the bad news."

I gave the kids another look, not displeased at how quiet they were being. They didn't stop eating, but each acknowledged me in their own way. Dylan stuck his tongue out at me, and Emily rolled her eyes.

"You mean that you want to drink," Emily clarified, after wiping her own face.

"I mean I want to look at the plans," I retorted, indignant.

I raised one of this body's eyebrows, like I had practiced.

"And drink," I finished. "What's wrong with that?"

She giggled, at this body's tone or its face.

"Drinking is icky," she said.

This body's eyes went wide, and I forgot in my passion for the drink that I was talking to a child. And that her parents were right there.

"Oh, no," I protested. "Drinking is good for the soul. Everyone has a taste and a buzz that suits them perfectly, and it's really up to each of us to find it."

It all came into focus, then.

"I mean, unless you're a kid," I said. "Then, yeah. Drinking is icky."

Henry exchanged a glance with Stephanie, and I didn't miss it.

"Sorry, guys," I said. "I don't meet a lot of kids in my line of work."

They laughed, together.

"It's okay, Ring," Henry said. "We forget sometimes too."

"Right?" I sputtered. "It's like they're whole people, but we can't treat them that way just yet."

I gave them once last look before I got up to help clear the dishes.

"Sorry, kids," I shrugged.

XXII.

It was not easy to coax Henry into drinking with me, after dinner. At some point I may have reminded him that he didn't have much time left, which wasn't really fair; but I do so hate to drink alone.

"I put in for more time off," he said, a few sips in. "Between now and the end of the year, I'm going to use all my vacation and sick days. Knowing what is coming is fine, but knowing I didn't take time to make peace with it first is not okay. I won't be telling Stephanie, and you won't either. Our routine is full of all the meaning I need, but I want to spend my days doing something else. Will you help me?"

I shrugged, glad I had insisted we stock his liquor cabinet. I made it look totally natural, opening a new bottle and pouring myself a generous helping. I made a big show off topping off his drink.

"It depends," I said. "Are you planning on murdering your enemies? Because I promised no killing, while I stay with you."

Henry chuckled.

"Jesus, Ring," he said. "Way to go all dark on me. No, I don't want to kill anyone. I don't even have any enemies. I'm a happy guy, buddy."

My laugh wasn't supposed to sound so bitter, or disbelieving; luckily, I could blame it on the scotch. Or this body. There were some seriously cynical thoughts buried in the brain I was thinking through, and they were bound to come out when my guard was down.

"Haven't you ever wondered?" I said, all low. "How it would feel to be someone's final struggle, to watch the light go out in their eyes? You can see the soul, if you're breathing right. It usually drifts—"

"Ring!" Henry was staring. "Enough, man. You're totally creeping me out. Lay off the death talk, would you? Until maybe New Year's?"

I waved my hand, finally feeling comfortable relaxing into this body's smile. Another sip of scotch accompanied the wave, and I kept the smile shining while I spoke.

"Of course!" I exclaimed. "Right, of course. So sorry. More scotch? So, I was thinking..."

I poured, while I talked.

"Instead of the guest room, I should stay out here," I said, still smiling. "This is a little more your space than the flowery spare room deco, and it's your space that I'm here to inhabit."

That gave him pause, and Henry stopped sipping to start talking.

"You're not..." he swirled the melting ice and friendly spirits. "You aren't going to take my place, are you? I mean, Stephanie..."

"Come on, Henry," I chided him. "Your wife is beautiful, but I'm not that guy. Your kids and your wife will be alone when you're gone, not haunted by some guy that looks like you but doesn't act like you."

He looked distressed, but not as distressed as when he was thinking of me married to his lady. Henry nodded, found a smile somewhere in his thoughts.

"Thanks, buddy," he said. "I think."

To change the colors swirling in the air, I shifted subjects.

"What are these plans, then?" I said. "These secret day plans?"

It was apparently something he had been thinking about quite a bit. Henry leaned forward, and kind of went off.

"I want to go hiking," he said. "And fishing, maybe. We won't put any bait on the line, so we don't have to explain the fish we don't bring home. Maybe a couple road trips, spending the day driving and listening to music I haven't heard in ages."

He looked at me.

"Doesn't that sound great?"

"Sure," I said, nodding and sipping between words. "All except the 'we' part. It sounds like you're just trying to include me, and really you don't have to."

I looked around the space, maybe for a little too long.

"Aw..." Henry laughed, and finished his scotch. "Are you looking forward to some time to yourself, Ring? How selfish of me, to think of my death when yours happens on a regular basis."

I sat up straight, and would have spilled my drink if there was any left. Waiting patiently while he filled it again, I frowned fiercely when he was finished.

"I'm not even mortal," I hissed. "I never die."

Henry shook his head, doggedly, and I realized I had gotten him drunk. Again.

"You never live, either," he said. "You never get to have a family, or get used to a routine, or pursue some desire of your own. Don't you ever get tempted, to stay with a family like mine and just live?"

It didn't matter how much I drank; I wasn't the one

who needed to find his way up the stairs. I tipped the bottle, had some more.

"No, Henry," I said, pretty clearly. "It isn't really an option. As soon as you're gone, I'll be drawn immediately to somewhere. I'll hear some other ringing. I'll go there, dressed in what looks like you, and ring in someone else."

Keeping his back straight and his eyelids propped completely open had become mutually exclusive tasks for Henry. Alternating between one and the other, as well as he could, he pressed on.

"Dressed in what looks like me?" he frowned, while smiling a little at the same time. "And where will I be?"

I shrugged.

"Well, technically," I said, "you'll be me, at least as far as universal records are concerned. Once the next service I have to perform is discharged, your soul will go back on the books as you. When I die, as you. Does that all make sense, then?"

Henry had nodded off. I roused him, and pointed him in the general direction of the door. He didn't seem to have any trouble finding his way, and soon I was settling into my new space.

I'd have to keep it up better than the old one.

XXIII.

Sleeping in my clothes was not at all uncomfortable, compared to the discomfort of habitually inhabiting an unfamiliar body. Sometime in the night or wee morning hours, someone had thrown a blanket over me and put some pajamas on a nearby seat cushion. A fluffy robe was draped over the back of the seat, and slippers sat at its base. I donned the comfort wear and padded into the kitchen.

Stephanie was at the sink, cleaning up the last of what looked like breakfast dishes. She turned her head when I walked in, smiled and turned back to her task.

"Look who's up," she said.

I didn't have to see the smile on her face; I could hear it in her voice.

"Morning," I said. "Is that coffee I smell?"

She nodded, and bent to dry her hands.

"Yeah," she said. "Let me get you a cup."

"No, no," I waved her away. "I'll get it. If I'm going to be staying here, I don't want to be a burden. I want to be helpful, when I can."

Rather than start opening cupboards at random, I paused.

"If you could just point me to the coffee cups..."

She smiled, over her shoulder, and pointed. As I filled my cup, she placed the last dish into the drainer. Without missing a beat, she went from washing and drying her hands to opening a drawer and removing a small pad of paper. She set it on the counter and began opening cupboards, moving boxes and cans aside, and making notations.

I didn't see what I was looking for in the fridge, and she caught me staring helplessly into the cold container.

"Ring?" she said. "What do you need?"

"Uh..." I was trying to remember. "Whose creamer is this?"

"It's what I use," she said. "You're welcome to have some."

I frowned, still staring.

"Nah," I said. "Too sweet. How does Henry take his coffee?"

Stephanie laughed. "With butter."

"Oh." I frowned some more. "Half and half, that's what I'm looking for. There's no half and half in here, is there?"

She shook her head, wrote something on the paper.

"Milk it is, then," I grimaced. I poured, and drank. The clouds began to part.

"Hey," I said, putting it all together. "Are you making a shopping list? I need to get some things, I can pick up your stuff too. Just be as specific about what you need as you want me to be when I'm picking it out."

I could see her hesitating, before she tried to turn me down. A moment's relief washed over her features, to be replaced by the set determination that had shaped them a moment before.

"No, that's okay," she said. "Tell me what you need, and I can pick it up. You're a guest, not an errand boy."

Looking down at my comfy ensemble, sipping my coffee, I nodded.

"I feel like a guest," I said, "and I appreciate that. But I have little to nothing that I need to do today, other than run to the store. You probably have a whole list of things to do today. It seems kind of rude for you to take away my one activity, when you have so many."

She narrowed her eyes, judging whether or not she wanted to be manipulated in such a friendly fashion.

"Other than that," I added, "you're being the perfect host."

Stephanie put down her pen, and turned her full attention to me. Now the relief was clear on her face.

"Really?" she said. "You wouldn't mind? Don't you have to work?"

"Nah." I waved this body's hand, dismissively.

"If I worked every day," I said, "they would start expecting me to work every day. Nobody wants that."

Stephanie laughed, and turned back to her list.

"Henry is always home by six, and I'll be out and about off and on until three," she said. "I'll bring the kids home around four, but you can hide out in Henry's cave as long as you like. Did he give you a key? And the alarm code?"

"Yeah," I nodded, and sipped. "I'm all set."

She tore the page from the pad, and handed it over. I glanced at it, furrowed this body's brow.

"You forgot scotch," I said, as she stepped from the room.

Stephanie was back a moment later, with her purse in hand.

"Is there any chance," she said, rummaging through it, "that you are going to forget to pick up scotch?"

I shrugged.

"Probably not," I admitted. "Still, it's nice to have it on there. Also, if you're looking for money...I won't take it."

She held up paper bills right as I said it, and I shook this body's head to illustrate.

"Nope," I said. "I got this."

"At least take Henry's truck," she said.

I had another look at the list, nodded.

"I will," I said. "Maybe I'll hit that hardware shop, too."

XXIV.

Something told me to go to the hardware store first, some whispered intuitive or logical connection. It only made sense, since groceries are more time-sensitive than building supplies; but I prefer to think it was intuition, trying to keep me from being in that particular store at that exact time. Like icy prickles down my back, the warning came as I parked Henry's pickup in the lot.

It doesn't matter which it was, I suppose; I didn't listen, either way.

Going into the grocery store, I feel a wave of dizziness wash over me. This body has a little trouble seeing its way to a cart, but the hands finally find one. I hold onto it, although it feels as though I'm turning slow circles inside the unfamiliar skin. My whole attention is dedicated to hanging on to the cart and keeping this body's knees from buckling, and it's not feeling like quite enough.

They call it vertigo, and explain it with all kinds of words that don't make sense to me. I call it 'overlapping', because that's what it feels like whenever it happens to me. It feels like I'm over here, and this body is over there, and nothing I can do is making them occupy the same space. It feels like inharmony, or discordance, at a cellular level.

It feels like I'm ringing in myself, and doing an awful job of it at that.

I don't know how I remember feeling this before, when I can't remember when that might have been; but I know I've had enough thoughts about it to have a name for it, and enough emotional charge around the thoughts to carry them with me. Remembering to breathe is not the problem; it's the breathing itself I'm having difficulty with. It doesn't seem like everything is spinning; it seems like everything is fixed in place, and only I can't find a place to lock into. If I was spinning, I could adjust; if the world was spinning, I could cope...I always do. But this...this is like a balloon whose string has been cut, floating about the general vicinity of where it should be but never quite finding its way there.

The voice barely cuts through the fog, but I can hear it far off in the disconnected distance. It's female, and trying to be helpful, and I do my best to make out the words.

"Are you alright?" are the words, spoken with kindness.

Something about the voice is off; but something about the world is off, so I don't notice right away. Also, I'm having a quietly dramatic internal event. I do my best to reply, and match her kindness.

"I'm fine," I mutter.

I try to wave her off, but taking this body's hand from the cart handle is not such a good idea. I feel knees buckling, and put everything I have into breathing right and standing up straight. This body does not want to obey my commands, and I get an image of me standing outside of it and shouting at it to move and breathe.

It's not amusing to me, in the moment.

The voice comes at me again, and this time I place it.

"Ring," she says. "Take my hand."

This body's eyes go wide, though I still can't seem to

mentally assimilate their visual input. I close them, in hopes of stringing together the words I most want to say right now.

"Cassandra!" I hiss, shaking this body's head. "You stay away from me! Just...just...don't touch me!"

"Stop it, Ring." Her voice is still calm, and polite as can be. "I'm going to put my hand over yours now, and you're going to stay calm."

My first impulse is to flail about, or run like mad; neither thought makes this body move, and my protestation comes out as a muttered moan. A moment later there is sensation, and I feel this body's eyes blinking away the overlapping at last.

The first thing I regain control of is the head, and I turn it to look daggers at her. As soon as the settling in moves like a wave to the hand she's holding, I pull it away.

I barely grab the handle of the cart again, and it wobbles with my efforts. I have a brief glimpse of people walking by, and staring; then the walls start closing in again.

"Ring, please," she says. "You know how much you do so hate to make a scene. You need to relax, and let me help you."

I didn't like the way she said that at all, like she knew me and she knew how I would say it. Mine is a solitary life, with few moments of true aloneness; ringers don't have feathers, or flock together. We are the original fringe dwellers, shaping a world we can never truly be part of.

Despite my internal protestations, she was right. I do so hate to make a scene. When she put her hand over mine this time, I let her. When the feeling started to come back into this body, I got right on top of its breathing. When I started to see colors, I turned to get a good look at her.

And when the ringing started, everything went suddenly dark.

XXV.

The pajamas Henry loaned me were not really a loan, so much as a gift. If I would be staying here until he moved along, then he would likely not be getting them back. That's why I will refer to my pajamas, when I tell you what I woke up in. Other than that, I'm not clear on much of anything.

My first thought is panic, and I rush to the door and fling it open. Before I can apologize to Stephanie for not getting her items at the store, Henry calls out from the living room.

"Hey, Ring," he says. "You been lounging all day?"

While I gathered this body's thoughts, Stephanie answered for me.

"He went to the store, earlier," she said. "He took your truck."

Her attention moved to me, and she smiled. I tried not to panic, as I looked back in this body's mind for a memory of parking his truck in the drive. I smiled back, as genuinely as I could.

"Thanks," she said.

I nodded, still panicking quietly.

"I didn't see any dents or dings in it, when I pulled up," Henry said. "Maybe I should have looked closer."

The breath that came whooshing out of this body could not have been mistaken for anything but relief, but no one other than me seemed to notice. I looked around, trying to order my thoughts, and called out a suggestion to Henry. He came walking into the room as I did, and I kind of called out to his face.

"Time for a drink before dinner?"

He glanced at me like he was going to say something smarmy, until he saw the look in this body's eyes. Instead he raised an eyebrow, and had a look at the time display on the oven.

"Rough day?" he said.

I nodded.

"Alright." Henry nodded. "Honey, we'll be a minute."

Stephanie had her attention on dinner, and it looked like it would be awhile. She nodded, and spoke over her shoulder at us both.

"You've got about thirty of them," she said.

He gestured to the door I had just come out of. I turned, grateful, and whisked into the room. When Henry saw how quickly I poured the drinks, he looked a little alarmed.

"Ring," he said. "Did you kill someone?"

This body's hands were shaking, for some reason. It was a special challenge to coax the ice cubes from their tray. Henry reached past me, scooped out a small frozen handful, and dropped two in each of our glasses. I smiled, grateful, and drank.

"I didn't kill anyone," I said, after. "At least, I don't think so."

Henry sipped his own scotch, eyeballing me critically the whole time.

"That hardly puts me at ease," he muttered.

"I went to the store," I said, frowning to remember better. "I got disoriented, and I started feeling like I was overlapping. I was dizzy, and my vision started closing in on me. It was all I could do to keep ahold of the grocery cart, and anchor myself in this body. Then I—"

"Ring," Henry said, cutting me off. "You may have walked into a body that is agoraphobic. You might want to be careful about going out too much. That, or you had some kind of panic attack. Are you sure you're alright?"

I took advantage of his talking to have another strong and steady sip, but I was waving this body's hand in negation the entire time.

"No," I said, putting down the glass.

Ice cubes swam while Henry poured, and I talked.

"That's not it," I said. "It's what I call overlapping, and it happens to ringers all the time. It's like my body is over here..."

I gestured, to my left.

"...and I'm over there..."

I gestured again, to my right.

"...and I can't put the two together for some reason."

I sipped, and added, "also, I'm not a walk-in. I'm a ringer. We went over that, remember?"

Henry wasn't hitting the bottle as hard as I was, but it didn't seem to bother either of us.

"I thought you said you don't remember anything," he pointed out. "You said that every body is a new start for you, as far as memories go. You also said that ringers don't know other ringers, so how do you know what other ringers experience?"

I shrugged, and kept my alcohol intake consistent.

"I remember remembering," I said. "If that makes sense."

He shook his head, had a slow sip.

"No," he said. "It really doesn't."

My wild gesticulation nearly sent the ice in my glass sailing, and I got ahold of this body's breathing before I spoke again.

"Well, Henry," I said, "that's how it is. I do have someone that watches over me, kind of. All ringers do. They're administrators, they don't deal with mortals in any way."

He looked at me, his edges slightly blurred.

"Ring," he said. "Who is your administrator?"

I shrugged. "I don't remember."

"When is the last time you talked?"

I shrugged again.

"My phone was ringing, for awhile," I said. "It said I had messages, but when I checked I think they were gone."

I cocked this body's head to the side, trying to remember.

"Yeah," I said, and shrugged again. "I'm sure everything is fine."

I felt better, as I finished whatever drink I was on.

"We should go have some dinner," I said. "Yeah, dinner sounds good."

Henry looked as though he wanted to say something, but I breezed past him to open the door for him. Instead he nodded, and walked through it.

XXVI.

The weekend came soon enough, and I learned quickly that this body's hands were not suited to carpentry. Henry laughed when I struggled, and looked skeptical when I offered to do some of the cuts.

"Can you run a saw?" he asked. "You're having a good deal of trouble with the drill, buddy."

I liked it when he called me buddy. I wasn't going to say anything, but I did like it.

"I got this," I said, all confident.

There seemed to be nothing to it, making the nice straight line and then starting the nice clean cut. I took it slow at first, and really leaned away from the process. It was so easy, I pushed harder and faster almost immediately. The board got a little wobbly as it transferred its weight across the table, and I moved this body's hand to steady it.

A sudden moment of shocked clarity precedes the pain, and the blade cuts entirely through one of this body's fingers before I use that clarity to pull back. Bodily instinct tells me to jam the wound into the folds of my flannel, under the opposite arm; ringer instincts have me breathing calm and steady, and closing this body's eyes to better clear my thoughts.

I see it growing back, in the darkness; and I feel it growing back a moment later. The growing back is far more painful than the cutting off had been, but I shut that off as soon as I start feeling it. It doesn't take more than a minute or two, which turns out to be plenty of time for Henry to rush to my side and shut off the whirring blade. His arm is around this body's shoulders, and he's coaxing me to lean its weight on him. The words he speaks are heavy with concern.

"Aw, hell," he says. "I'm so sorry, Ring. Lean on me, buddy. We'll get you to an emergency room. I knew I shouldn't have let you use the saw."

I do lean into him, for a moment. As soon as he starts to lead me off, I step away and shake this body's head.

"It's okay," I say, pulling the hand from the bloody shirt.

I splayed the fingers of this body's hand, showing him that the offending digit had been replaced. Only blood remained, staining the skin and the flannel. Henry watched with wide eyes, and bent to pick up the collection of bone and blood and skin I had dropped in the grass. It was shorn off clean, and also stained red with this body's blood.

"Gross, Henry," I said. "Put that down. I don't need it any longer, either."

Despite my words, Henry held the thing up between us, pinching the severed finger between two of his own. His eyes went from the dead piece of flesh to this body's undamaged hand several times before he spoke.

"How did you..." he shook his head. "Really, Ring?"

I shrugged.

"I'm a ringer," I said. "It wouldn't do for me to get injured before I am done with this body. How am I supposed to complete my mission, if I am hurt or unconscious? This body is under my control, in all the ways it needs to be. Have I not explained that?"

Finally, he dropped the finger into the grass again.

I sighed, relieved to have it out of my line of sight.

Henry seemed to be having a moment, and I let him. After another moment passed, and he was still looking at me with that shocked expression, I feared that he might have slipped a cog or something. Then he shook off the look, and spoke quietly.

"I think I need a moment," he said, although I had just given him two. "This was all kind of fun when it was hypothetical, but now..."

His words drifted off, and I was afraid Henry might do the same.

"Don't be silly," I said, to keep him engaged. "You can hear the ringing, and you could feel our connection from the beginning. I even opened you up, and gave you a more expansive view of the system."

Henry nodded, not looking directly at me for some reason.

"You did," he said. "It wasn't all that different from what I've seen in meditation, though; and it faded, just the same."

"It did?" I ruffled this body's brow. "It shouldn't have. Come here, I'll give you another—"

"Don't, Ring," Henry said abruptly, taking a step back.

He looked at me then, warily.

"I don't have much time left in this life," he muttered. "Let me at least feel connected to it while I can."

I gave him his space, and he finally shared his thoughts.

"The ringing," he said, "it's proof, sure; but it's subtle proof. There has been a ringing in my ears many times in my life, and it never meant that my death was imminent. Our connection was obvious, but that's subtle as well. There was no logical explanation for why I would invite a stranger into my home, especially when I was pretty sure he had killed some folks at some point; but there it was, the proof of my own intuition."

There was some lawn furniture nearby, and Henry found a chair and sat down. I pulled another up next to him, and sat as well. I was glad he was talking, instead of shutting down.

"The awakening thing," he went on. "That was pretty impressive stuff, and I have never had another person affect me that way. Still, it was not what one would call physical evidence."

He glanced in the direction of the finger, still lying in the cut grass. I wish he wasn't so on top of his yard work; it would have been better if it had disappeared in overgrown greenery. If either of us wanted to see the bloody disconnected digit, all we had to do was look down. I didn't want to, but I could see that Henry did. While he stared at it, he spoke quietly.

"It's real proof, Ring," he said. "I'm going to die soon."

XXVII.

Neither one of us heard her step outside, and Stephanie was pretty much right on top of us before either Henry or I registered her approach. There was no time to move, or react at all, before she did.

To her credit, she didn't scream.

She did let out a shocked little hiccup, before she looked us both up and down. Her eyes settled on the blood that had stained my flannel, and she moved in close to get a good look at my hands.

"Ring," she said. "What happened? Are you alright?"

I gave her a friendly little wave, to show her all of this body's fingers.

Her eyes were going back and forth between the blood and the offending digit, as she tried to put it all together. She looked at Henry, but he wouldn't meet her gaze. When she spoke, her eyes were on mine.

"Is this a joke?" she said. "Because it isn't funny."

She moved toward the finger, where it lay in the grass, and bent to pick it up. Now Henry moved, and spoke; as did I.

"Honey, don't..." Henry said, standing beside his chair.

"Not a good idea..." I said, at the same time.

I remained seated.

Nonetheless, she picked it up. I imagine it was still pretty warm, and wet, and soft to the touch; from the way she reacted, it felt like a finger to her.

"That's real!" she exclaimed, dropping it to the ground again.

Henry looked at me, to keep from meeting her eyes. I got the message: if anyone was going to lie to her, it would have to be me.

"Stephanie," I said, "it was a joke, but it was a joke on Henry. You weren't supposed to see it, or be upset by it. I do apologize."

She shook her head, adamant.

"Don't lie to me, Ring," she said. "That finger is real."

I didn't want to put Henry on the spot, but I couldn't come up with any explanation for an actual finger. A bad joke, I could explain; a detached digit was beyond me, in the moment.

When I looked his way, she did too. Henry met both of our gazes before he shook his head, and rested his eyes on the ones I was looking out of.

"Sorry, buddy," he said. "You've got to tell her."

The whirling thoughts pick me up and spin me around suddenly, and I can't decide whether to whirl away with them or get ahold of them. Stephanie and Henry are both looking at me; and I'm not sure if he thinks I have some story to tell, or if he really expects me to blow my own cover. Out of the blue, or the distant past, a thought comes along to put all the whirling to rest.

"It's okay, Henry," I say, breathing once more. "If you want her to know, then she can know. It will make this whole experience different for all of us, but it's okay. As long as you both know that she will forget, after I am gone. Ringers can interact with people that they aren't ringing, in special cases like these, I believe. They just forget what they learn, after they lose contact with the ringer and the...well, you know. The person the ringer is ringing."

That didn't seem to settle either one of them down. Stephanie looked more confused than before, and maybe a little hurt as well. Henry was glaring, and looked like he wanted to start yelling. Instead he spoke calm and clear, in a tone that kind of made me wish that he had picked the yelling.

"What do you mean?" he said. "It's okay if she knows? I didn't have to keep this from her at all? That's been the hardest part of this whole thing, Ring; you know that. Why would you not tell me that she—"

"What are you talking about?!"

Stephanie's verbal explosion silenced both Henry's barrage and my readied response. Rather than crackle with ice or burn with righteous anger, her tone spoke of that hurt I thought I had seen a glimpse of a moment earlier. It made Henry and I turn together, and start to answer.

She held up a hand, to silence us both again.

"No offense, Ring," she said, "but shut up."

I nodded, spread this body's fully fingered hands in surrender.

She put her eyes and attention on Henry.

"You, I know I can trust," she said. "Start talking."

I'm not sure if Henry would have shot me a panicked look then, if I hadn't told him it was okay for her to know a minute before. Something told me that it didn't matter, that he would have told her everything at any point if she had realized something was up and confronted him; it had been tortured pain for him to simply have a thought he couldn't share with her, and it was a special kind of gratifying to watch the tension relax as he prepared to unburden himself.

Rather than listen to him, at first, I thought of how maybe the things that hurt us are the things that eventually kill us; I mean...not us, but people. Maybe the reason that a ringer doesn't age is because a ringer cannot love; not really, anyway. Any pain or pleasure we experience is lost and forgotten the moment we don a new skin, and love between two people is just a certain collection of those pains and pleasures. No matter how transcendental my hurt, no matter how encompassing my happiness, it is all but momentary memories to be forever forgotten.

It was too deep, and too sad. Instead, I focused on the actual love that these actual people were able to experience, and I tuned in to listen to what Henry had to say about what he knew.

My pocket started vibrating, which made me wonder when I had put a phone in there; that made me wonder who would have charged the phone I brought with me, or why anyone including me would put it in my pocket...

And that, all together, made it easy to ignore.

XXVIII.

Shortly after Henry started talking, Stephanie settled her weight in the lawn chair he had just stood up from. I remained seated, and from time to time she looked at me for confirmation of the story Henry was telling her. My way has always been to throw the person wide open, and then explain the details to their freshly blown mind; his was gentle, and careful, and quite a bit less potentially misleading.

"Ring is not who he says he is," Henry told her, "and he's not who I have been saying he is either. I mean, he is a friend; but he isn't some guy that happened to move into the neighborhood recently. There's a reason he looks the way he does, and there's a quickly disappearing trail of how he got here, but the important thing is the reason that he is here. Ring is here to help me. You could say he's kind of like an angel that—"

I started to protest, but Henry waved me off.

"I said 'kind of like an angel'," he said. "Relax."

"He's a ringer," Henry went on. "He comes to the aid of the kind of people who need him, and the kind of people who need him are the ones who need to put their affairs in order. Ring is here to help me see how important everything I have is, and then help me transition out of this life. He's more than a friend; he's like a guardian for my soul."

Stephanie looked to me, and I nodded. It's not the way I would have put it, but that didn't mean I didn't like it. Maybe I would remember that point of view, when I looked at this whole ringing business through Henry's eyes.

I hoped so.

"It's been hard," Henry continued, "knowing that the end was near, and not being able to tell you. I have been more present in my moments with you, for knowing it, and it isn't fair that you didn't have that same opportunity. I'm so sorry for keeping this from you."

They were looking deep into each other's eyes as he spoke, him standing next to her chair and her looking up at him. I was beginning to feel a little awkward, and the feeling increased exponentially when he dropped to one knee beside her. If it had been a movie I was watching, I would have been touched; sitting in the lawn chair beside her felt a little like I was imposing. I was considering getting up, and getting lost, when they both turned to look at me.

"You told me she couldn't know," Henry said. "What gives? Why the change of heart?"

I shrugged, and avoided both of their gazes.

"I remembered," I said. "I remembered that there are special cases, where people that aren't part of the ringing can know about it, kind of."

"What do you mean, kind of?" Henry pressed me.

"And, what exactly is ringing?" Stephanie wondered, aloud.

His question was much easier to answer, and I would let him fill her in on what he thought of this process later on. It was bound to be quite a bit more considerate of how it would affect her than my way might be.

"She'll forget," I said, simply. "She won't remember

anything she learns about ringing, or ringers, after I am gone."

Henry stood up again, and loomed over me.

"She'll forget?" he demanded. "What will she forget? Some of the final moments of my life, some of the things I want her to remember most? What were you thinking, Ring? Why didn't you tell me that?"

I shook my head, and locked this body's eyes on his to show that I was being sincere.

"I tried," I said, and went on to try to explain. "She won't forget it all, anyway. Just the conversations we have about why I am actually here in your lives. Like the majority of words exchanged between folks in casual conversation, those words will be lost. The connections they made possible will be lost with them, and no one will be damaged or left incomplete for that loss. That's not the way the system works, Henry; it's all geared to protect people from knowing everything there is to know all at once. When that happens we either stop playing the game, or master it; and then it's time for a new game."

Stephanie was handling this all very quietly, though I suspected there would be at least one talk that lasted long into the night in their near future. With them, it caused me no worry; they were the type of people to heal pain rather than live with it, and they would be closer for enduring the pain of that healing together.

Even if it ended in Henry dying.

She spoke now, and the kindness in her voice made me glad we had brought her into the circle.

"As long as I remember our time together," she said, "I know I can handle anything. It's almost like our life together has been one long loving exercise in you building up my reserves, so I could never run out of love. Maybe this is why."

She was looking into Henry's eyes again, her head tilted back to gaze up at him. When she turned to me, I could see tears glistening in her eyes.

"I will remember you, won't I?" she asked. "My husband's mysterious best friend who showed up out of nowhere to make his last days even more meaningful, and then disappeared as mysteriously as he showed up? Will I remember a little, at least?"

I nodded.

"You'll remember a lot," I said. "They'll be good memories, too, that will help you after Henry and I are both gone."

They gazed into each other's eyes again, and I don't know if either of them heard what I said after that.

"I won't, of course," I muttered. "I won't remember anything."

<h1 style="text-align:center">XXIX.</h1>

Once everything was explained to her momentary satisfaction, Stephanie showed us both yet another good reason to be thoroughly impressed with her. She went to the finger, picked it up and took it inside. While she was walking away, she called back softly over her shoulder.

"See, honey?" she said. "It's a good thing we got the heavy duty garbage disposal, instead of the cheap midline one. I'm going to get rid of this, so we don't find a dog chewing on it later or a kid making it into a good luck charm."

I watched Henry watch her walk away. It was one of the most completely sublime spectacles I had ever seen.

"She's pretty great," I said. "Hang on to that one, Henry."

He shot me a stern look, but his eyes had a playful twinkle. For a moment, he considered something. Then he smiled a little, and spoke.

"For what?" he said. "The next thirteen days?"

"Thirteen?" I sat upright; that had to be wrong. "What's the date?"

Henry laughed, and this time the bitterness was tingeing the humor.

"It's the eighteenth, Ring," he said. "Christmas is next weekend, and New Year's is the weekend after that."

I quailed a little, inside, and tuned into the ringing in

a way that I apparently hadn't in days. He was right; it was getting louder, and we only had a couple weeks left.

"You haven't taken any extra time off," I said. "You were going to take some extra time off."

I'm not the kind of fellow that takes special note when another fellow is particularly handsome. It made sense that I would notice, when Henry was at his best; I would be as handsome as him soon, and in the same way. This body looked most appealing when I thought dark thoughts, or frowned fiercely, or when I just relaxed its features deliberately. In thirteen days, my features would look their best when I was being thoughtful, or nostalgic; I both looked forward to that, and didn't.

"I'm going to take time off," Henry said. "Now that I can tell Stephanie, I won't feel bad while I'm doing it. Maybe she'll even spend some time with me, now that she knows."

"She probably will," I said, "if you ask. She'll probably understand if you want to have some time to yourself, too. You know I do. She can certainly have my days, if you would rather spend them with her. Like I told you before, I feel particularly at home in my current quarters."

He was being thoughtful again, and looking all handsome for it. It would be worth thinking of others, if I could look that good when I did. Of course, the thoughts would fade, along with the memories of those thoughts...but what harm could there be in thinking of others, from time to time?

"You don't have much time left, either," he said. "I'm sorry, buddy. I hope you have found some measure of peace here with us, and that it lasts for you somehow."

His eyes burned with the love of a truly good soul, as Henry locked them on me. I couldn't imagine how Stephanie must have felt, all those years ago, when he professed his love and began to show his dedication; but I could imagine how a pretty lady might feel, with me on the other side of those beaming blue eyes, and acting all sensitive.

"You're a very odd duck," he went on, "but I couldn't be more grateful that it was you who came along to help me through this. Thanks, buddy. You made me see that it's better to have a meaningful death now than a shocking or surprising one later. Knowing can probably be a blessing or a curse, and you surely know that better than I do; but I see it as a blessing, the same way as I see you."

If you fling insults at me, I can stand there and take them all day. I don't like to, and I'll walk off or take you out if I can; but if I'm in for a verbal beating, I can bear up just fine. Toss a compliment my way, though, and I've got no option other than getting all flambustergated and evasive.

"Aw, shucks, Henry," I said. "Thanks. You're an odd duck, too."

He wouldn't let me slip out of it, and I vacillated between discomfort and a warm glow while he insisted.

"I'm serious," he said. "Not many people get this chance, and I'm grateful for it. I'm grateful for you, and our friendship. Get over your blustery self and accept it for what it is, buddy; I'm grateful to the system, for you. For this. I can't think of a better way to pass through the doorway that I'll be passing through, and I can't think of anyone I'd rather have accompany me to that doorway than you."

Stephanie came out again then, and I was relieved to derail the uncomfortable path our conversation had taken.

"Did that finger grind up okay?" I called out, quietly, when she was within earshot.

She gave me a thumbs-up, and nodded.

My phone was ringing again, buzzing in my pocket, and I dutifully ignored the potential interruption.

I was having too good of a day, for that.

XXX.

I can't say whether or not I've ever been on skis, in any body; but I know the snowboards at the rental shop have me visualizing myself healing broken limbs all day. It would only make sense, that this body had skied before. It went with the suits, and the scotch, and the murders.

Or had those been me?

It was hard to tell, and it didn't matter with the cold wind rushing against this body's face. There was a special thrill in feeling in control and out of it all at once...do one thing wrong with this body, and I'd dump it in powder; but keep it together, and it was a kind of freedom that felt like it could be addicting. Lining up the skis and blazing down the mountain in a straight line had me on the verge of mad giggles every time.

Then, there are the other bodies. The ones on skis seem pretty predictable, but the ones on boards seldom seem to be going the direction they should be. Both examples are all over the slopes, in every stage of ability imaginable. I'm good enough to stay up, pretty much right away; after a while, I'm ready to move on to longer runs. At no point am I nimble enough to avoid someone boarding right at me, and that's just what happens on my fourth good run.

I think I'm moving along at a pretty good clip, until the

lightning blue blur comes out of nowhere and topples me bodily. It's not like I lose my balance; I'm literally knocked off this body's feet, and my skis fly while I tumble to a stop in the snow. The body that smashed into this one rolls with me a couple times, and I hear it cry out. It's a woman, or a man that sounds pretty girlie when he yells. That deflates my anger a little, before I even come to a complete halt.

There won't be the satisfying crack of one angry dude slugging another, but that doesn't mean I won't be giving her a good scolding.

Just as soon as I can find my feet, and a way to walk with this body's ankles locked in place.

Which, it turns out, is not so simple.

I feel like I'm practicing marching in place, and I imagine it looks even more silly than it feels. It's really more wobbling in place than walking, and I'm glad that one of my poles didn't go flying off or sliding down the mountain. Actually, it's all pretty close by: while I do the awkward march of the skier without skis, she fetches all of my lost items. When she comes and sticks them in the snow at my feet, along with her board, she is already apologizing when she reaches up to pull her bright blue scarf from her face. I peel up the ski mask I'm wearing at the same time, and we realize together.

"Ring!" she says, smiling.

"Cassandra!" I hiss, pulling the wool back over this body's eyes. I adjust it until I can see, although I am not at all keen on what I'm seeing.

"What a coincidence," she says, still smiling.

My breathing isn't exactly the slow steady effortless expansiveness it was a minute ago; the world has gone from sharp and scintillating colors to shades of dull gray, and it was making me suddenly aware of the numbing cold.

"Yeah," I muttered, through the fabric. "Coincidence. Right."

"Are you here by yourself?" she asked.

The question sounded rhetorical, which bothered me. Was she assuming I was always alone, or that I never was? Either way, the way she asked kind of irked me.

"My friends are black diamond people," I said, in the most dismissive tone I could muster. "And I like to ski alone."

I reached out, to grab the other pole; she reached out at the same time, for her board. I thought she was making a move, to seize me for some reason, and I drew back. Of course, I lost my balance; and I fell.

She moved forward, to help me. I skittered backwards on the snow, more awkward than ever in the confining footwear. Finally, she stood and put her hands on her hips.

"Fine," she said. "Don't accept my help. Unfasten the top buckles on your boots, and you'll be able to stand up easier."

Bending to attach her board to her feet once more, Cassandra ignored my snowy struggle until I managed to regain this body's feet. She was right, the ability to move its ankles made it a lot easier; but there was no need to thank her, since she was what kept knocking me down. Before drifting away, she gave me one last long look.

I couldn't tell if it was judgment or real concern I saw in her eyes, but I know what my intuition was screaming at me.

I looked away, made a big show of arranging my skis.

"You know, Ring," she said, "you're a real piece of work."

As soon as I knew she wasn't watching to see if I was watching her, I started watching her disappear down the mountain.

All of the sudden, I wasn't in the mood for skiing anymore at all.

XXXI.

There's enough in the black label bottle to keep me warm the rest of the day, and I don't even have to ask the bartender if he has a backup. The lodge is not exactly the kind of place that I or this body would likely frequent, but it was better than literally running into that woman again.

Coincidence. Right.

I asked the bartender to change the channel, as soon as I sat down. He glanced at the big screen, shrugged, and nodded noncommittally.

"Sure," he said. "To what?"

"I don't know," I shrugged back. "Anything but American football?"

I probably should have considered the fact that there was really no one but him around, and that the station selection had likely been his in the first place. All I got was a dirty look, and a double that looked like a single the next time I asked for a drink.

Oh, and a football game...American style, of course.

It seemed like a good time to fiddle with my phone, until I remembered that I had quite distinctly made it a point to leave it behind; then it seemed strange that I should be holding it, and looking at it, when I shouldn't have had it with me at all. Even though I hadn't been charging it, there was a little group of numbers on the screen telling me it had a full charge.

Speaking of full charge…I got another double that looked like a single, and considered doubling down on the singles to start getting more generous pours.

A little icon of what phones used to look like is on the dashboard, and there is an exclamation point attached to it instead of a number. I tap the image, and a blank screen shows up. There are no voicemails, or texts, or numbers to call back.

Not that I would have; I was just checking to see who wanted to talk to me so badly that they wouldn't stop calling. I switch over to the keypad, and input a series of nines. When I hit 'call', I have no idea what's going to happen. I sip at my scotch, and put the device to this body's ear.

It rings, but it sounds like a dull and far off sound. I try to increase the volume, but it just sounds like a dull and far off sound that has been amplified. Then it stops ringing, and my heart starts pounding.

"This number is for emergency calls only," a voice says, clearly.

The sound is so loud, after I had cranked the volume, it sets this body's heart to beating even faster. I can't tell if the voice is male or female, it's wound up so tight. All I can say is that it sounds like a voice that's accustomed to yelling at folks, and having them do what they're told. I'm sure it's a recording, which is why I don't respond.

"Is this an emergency call?"

I'm startled all over by the follow-up question, and I sneak a look at the bartender like I think he can hear both ends of the conversation and my thoughts somehow. He's cleaning glasses, and leaving spots.

"Well, no," I say, gathering my wits at last. "This is not

an emergency call. Sorry to bother you."

I pull the phone away from this body's face, and can hear the voice coming back again as its finger hovers over the screen.

"Ring?" The voice sounds kind now, and anxious.

I think it's a guy.

"Ring?" he says again. "Is that you?"

"Sorry," I say. "Wrong number."

After touching the disconnect icon, I throw back the rest of my drink. It goes down too easily, probably because it's mostly melted ice at this point. The phone starts vibrating as soon as I set it on the bar, and I ignore it to catch the bartender's attention.

"Hey," I say, waving and giving him a most friendly smile. "Can I buy you a drink?"

He grunts, and it sounds like it's an affirmative sound.

"One for me, too," I say, in case it wasn't implied. "Doubles, both."

He sets two glasses in front of me, and pours exactly the same amounts of two very different whiskies into them. The cheap sonofabitch doesn't even know how to give himself a generous pour, apparently. We sit across from each other for a very uncomfortable minute, drinking, until I put more money on the bar and ask for another.

When he sets it down, he glances at my phone. It's still buzzing intermittently, dancing across the bar in tiny increments with each buzz.

"Wife?" he sneers.

I look at him, and then the phone; I shake my head.

"No," I say. "No wife."

He nods, like he knows or something.

"Work?"

I frown, and nod.

"Yeah, work," I say.

"Why don't you shut it off?" Still sneering.

"I can't."

The scotch tasted better with my thoughts than it does with his.

"Important call, huh." He says it like it isn't even a question.

"No," I say. "I literally can't."

Suddenly the padded contest on the screen is much more interesting. I focus on it, and ignoring him.

Eventually, he goes away.

XXXII.

It isn't fun at all, to have them pressing me while I'm in the back seat trying to enjoy this body's buzz. Henry keeps looking in the rearview, and Stephanie is constantly turning around in her seat to look his way or mine. I'm feeling pinned down, and finding it difficult to sip at my flask when neither of them has eyes on me.

"Are you sure you're okay, buddy?"

Henry has asked me that a half dozen times already; I don't know why, since I keep giving him the same answer.

"I'm fine, Henry," I say, like I did before.

They exchange a look, again; during which I sip at my flask, again.

The flask is in my lap when Stephanie turns, out of her line of sight.

"Henry's worried about you," she says. "And so am I."

I smile, and nod.

"That's sweet, you two," I say. "And totally unnecessary."

While they glance each other's way, I have a good long pull.

"Actually," I say, "it's also kind of ridiculous. You find out that I'm an immortal, and you start clucking around me like mother hens. Isn't that backwards? Once you saw this body's finger grow back, shouldn't you have ceased worrying about me completely?"

I held up the evidence, showing them the perfect hand and hiding the next sip. It was a small sip; we had a ways to go yet.

Stephanie was almost all the way backward, pivoting to face me more fully, before she spoke.

"Henry told me about your episode," she said.

I looked at her, confused. I caught Henry's eyes in the rearview, and watched his shoulders lift and drop in a subtle shrug.

"At the store," Stephanie said, like it meant something.

When they exchanged another look, I saw the kindness in it. Henry held my eyes in the mirror, although he spoke to her.

"His memory, honey," he said. "It's not so good."

I waved this body's hand, forgetting that there was an open container in it. A little splashed on the seat, while I made my case.

"My memory is fine," I snapped. "It just wasn't an episode, okay? There are aspects of ringing that neither of you understand, that no one but a ringer can understand. I'm fine. Do you understand that?"

They exchanged another look, and we drove in silence for awhile. When Henry sniffed at the air, and looked her way again, I held up the flask.

"Yeah," I said. "I'm drinking whisky. I may have spilled a little. Sorry about that."

Stephanie was facing forward, watching the road. They were both quiet, and didn't look at me, for another minute.

"It's okay, buddy," Henry said, after awhile.

He caught this body's eyes in the rearview, and smiled.

"You can talk to us, you know," he said.

"Yeah, Ring." Stephanie turned in her seat again.

"What happened back there at the mountain? You seemed pretty upset when we met up in the lodge."

Now that it was out in the open, I sipped the flask for all to see.

"That guy was pouring thimble shots," I frowned. "And watching football. I think I hate football. I definitely hate that guy."

Stephanie shook her head.

"You had been drinking for awhile, from the look of it," she said. "What happened? Why did you stop skiing? It looked like you were having so much fun when we left you."

I nodded.

"I was," I said.

"Did you have another episode?" she asked, kindly.

I shook this body's head, had another sip, capped the flask and stowed it in my jacket.

"I did not have a first episode," I said. "So I could not have had another episode. I just felt like drinking, more than skiing. Is that okay?"

I caught Henry's eye in the rearview, smirked.

"Dad?" I said, and turned to her. "Mom? Is that okay?"

Henry's eyes were on the road again, and his voice sounded much more calm than mine had.

"It's okay, Ring," he said. "It's okay if the wide open space of the mountain triggered another panic attack, too. We get that you're immortal, but that doesn't mean you are without issues. We're your friends, buddy. You can talk to us about—"

"Fine," I snapped, cutting him off. "There was a woman, at the store. She has been everywhere, at the bus stop and the store and the airport. She acts like she knows me, or something. For some reason I can't explain, she makes me feel terrified just by being nearby."

I remembered, as I reached for the flask again.

"Stephanie met her," I said. "When we ran into each other at the store, before I came to stay with you guys."

It was hard to catch her eye, unless she turned to look at me. For some reason she was watching the road intently, not even glancing at Henry.

"Remember?" I said. "Stephanie? The woman you met?"

She looked at Henry, briefly; then her eyes found the road again.

I shook my head, sipped the scotch.

"She keeps turning up," I went on. "I have seen her every time I've gone out in public, and this was no exception. She literally ran into me, knocked me right off my skis, and then tried to act all friendly-like. I don't know what her game is, but I know I don't want to play it."

Henry nodded, a little too triumphantly.

"I knew something was wrong," he said. "Don't you feel better, talking about it? Honey, you remember that woman? Didn't you say she seemed interested in Ring?"

Stephanie looked at him, her brow furrowed. She glanced back at me, and shook her head.

"I remember running into Ring," she said. "But he was alone. I don't remember any woman."

When Henry caught this body's eyes in the mirror, I let him see that I did not feel better for having talked. I felt more perplexed and frustrated than before, and the last of the whisky didn't seem to help the feeling at all. I stowed the empty container in my inside pocket, leaned back and closed this body's eyes.

The sleep that came for me was neither peaceful nor refreshing, but at least it put an end to the conversation I didn't want to have.

XXXIII.

Everywhere else, this body feels like an uncomfortable suit that moves along slightly out of step with my thoughts. Even at the dinner table, with the soft comforting colors drifting everywhere, I feel a touch of the discomfort. It's only here, in Henry's simple man cave, that I feel as though this body and I are one. I know it isn't true, but it's still nice to feel that way.

In this room, with a couple drinks in me, everything seems like it might just work out all right. I'm not sure if I am forgetting that there is really no end to all this, or if I'm feeling okay with my own eternal nature on a deeper level.

The best way to stick with the feeling is to not think about it.

It's as though the opposite is true for Henry: everywhere else, he is the picture of calm and consideration. Here, he lets the anxiety of the impending situation hit him.

It's a nice balance, I think.

"This used to be such a place of peace, for me," Henry says, giving voice to the tension I see in him. "Now I feel like it's a constant reminder of the fact that I only have a few days left. It feels silly, to try to refresh myself, when life won't need me any more so soon. I should be relaxed and at peace, especially here. But this is where it all hits me."

I nodded, trying to impart some of my calm to him.

"That's healthy," I said. "Part of being a man is keeping it together; and part of keeping it together is having a place to fall apart. This is where you have always come, to defragment your mind in a sense. But there's no dealing with death, except by walking through that doorway; there is no peace in accepting the end of everything you have known and loved, unless it's something you have longed to let go of for some time."

Shaking his head, sipping his scotch, Henry frowned.

"I can't understand that," he mused. "As much as I love to dwell in the presence of my soul, I do it to strengthen my ability to show up in my own life. Meditation has never made me long for an end to anything, and even that thing you did with my third eye didn't make me want to pass on. If anything, it made me feel more connected with my life; not less."

I nodded, not bothering to correct him again about the whole third eye thing. If Henry wanted to get it wrong, that was his business.

"It wasn't supposed to detach you from your life," I said. "It was meant to make you more aware of your own soul, and its continuity. This life is a part of that continuity. You'll take it with you when you go, in your own way. You'll keep it with you always."

We exchanged a look, and I could see that Henry was holding his tongue. I said it for him.

"Unlike me," I shrugged.

"That's not true," Henry said. "Or, at least you don't know it for sure. Every soul has a path, and a purpose, from what you say you believe."

I let a smile spread across this body's face.

"Belief has nothing to do with it," I said. "Life is. What's to believe?"

Henry took the time to refill both our glasses, and drop

another cube of ice into each of our drinks.

"Alright," he said. "Life is, and life never abandons life. There is no way for you to exist, unless you are on a path of your own, according to your definition of the way life is."

I shook my head.

"That's the way life is for you," I said. "And for others within the system. I work outside the system, and the rules don't apply to me in the same way. My soul is a patchwork piece, an afterthought created when the system saw its own shortcoming. I'm not made of the same stuff as other souls."

Henry watched me carefully while I drank.

"There is nothing outside the system," he mused. "You said so yourself. You also said you've been around since the beginning. Which is it, then?"

"It's neither," I waved my empty glass, to call attention to it. "It's both. I don't know how I'm supposed to explain the system, when I don't understand it myself. I just know I'm not part of it, at least not the way mortals are. I'm not the car or the road or the map or the journey, Henry. I'm just the grease in someone's wheels, then the gas in someone else's tank. Once I have burned off, for them, we both forget who I was as we move on in different directions. There is no path, no lesson and no continuity in that. Trust me, I know."

We sit in silence so long that I finally glance his way, to see him deep in thought. I sip, placid to my core, and watch him think.

After a few minutes, he speaks.

"Will it hurt?" he asks.

Henry looks at me, to let me see the stark vulnerability in his questioning eyes.

I shake my head.

"No, buddy," I say, quietly. "It won't hurt at all. I'll make sure of it."

XXXIV.

Henry decided to surprise his folks, and Stephanie's, and take a trip to the bay area for Christmas. I knew it was with me in mind, and my desire to drink up the peace of his space; I knew it especially because he provided me with a number of bottles, and no need to venture out. It left me with the house to myself, and opportunity to hole up for a couple days with this body's spinning mind.

As much as I've tried to keep it at bay, this face has started to resemble Henry's more and more as the day draws nearer. It's hard to look in the mirror, without seeing him there. Stephanie must have noticed, even if Henry hadn't; but neither of them had said anything, and I was glad for it.

I still couldn't decide if I liked looking at the reflection, or hated it.

I practiced staring at the phone for awhile, wondering why it only rang when I didn't feel like talking. The messages were still not there, and there was no real proof that they ever had been. Once this face had changed completely, so would the memory of messages unread.

How is that a teachable moment, when I forget everything I learn?

Maybe some thoughts are like mulch, turning from

excrement to new ideas as they rot; maybe, also, they're best left unremembered.

There is a recording on the phone, although I don't know if it's got anything to do with me. I listen to it, and find that it does. I listen to it again, and once more, before I close the app and let it drift finally from my thoughts.

There is, of course, no way I'm calling that number again.

Maybe Henry is right. There's no reason for my morose demeanor if there's nothing cooking below the surface. Why would I love the drink so much, if I wasn't fermenting something myself? I wondered aloud, and even asked the empty bottle; but no answer was forthcoming.

Somehow, I was not surprised.

I opened another, perhaps looking more deeply for answers or more fervently for numbness. Perhaps in one, I might find the other.

I brighten when I realize that I will be Henry soon. Other than some lingering desire to be a good father and husband, I shouldn't be haunted by much of anything. I've rung him in enough to know that I should spend a few minutes canceling what little party plans I've made. There will be no gathering, and not much drinking either. Even my own desire has transformed, to capture a buzz rather than smash my thoughts.

Luckily, I'm fighting it for now.

At least I'll still like scotch. Thank the system for that.

I find myself watching a little news, and reading some of Henry's new age books. Mostly, I spend time waiting for his family to come home and warm the spaces between the walls again. It's nice to wait, and make it seem as though I am making the moments longer by watching them go by.

After listening to the recording once more, I think it might be a good idea to leave myself another. It will be

Henry's ears that hear it, in a sense; but I'm the one that will have to take the action.

"Ring," I say, into the mobile device.

I watch the meter dance, while I talk to myself.

"It's me," I say. "Or you, before you rang this guy that you look like in. There are some things you should know, and some things you should do, after you have become Henry."

I go on, watching the electronic waves.

"You need to get out of town," I say. "You can't be running into his wife, or his kids. Also, some woman has been lurking about. Her name is Cassandra. Watch out for her. She seems to mean you no good, so far as I can tell. Relocating might get you off her radar."

I thought for a few seconds, watched the meter level out while the timer ticked on.

"Maybe Venice Beach," I said. "Or Santa Cruz. I'm thinking it might be time to try being a beach bum. It seems like maybe we have fond memories of that, or have always wanted to do it. Whatever you do, don't take from this guy or his family. They've been real friends, and the money in your pocket is enough to get you where you need to go."

I nodded, and added one final thought.

"You're a ringer," I said. "Remember, the system always provides for ringers. Have faith, and do good with your new body."

I sighed. "Henry would have."

While I've still got it in me, I set out to tie one on real good before they come home. I've only got a week left; and for some reason, it feels like I'm the one that will be passing on.

XXXV.

The family returned, and the final countdown began. Henry and I worked feverishly on the little structure in the backyard, and I learned quickly as these hands began to work more like his. He commented, finally, on how much I was beginning to ring in his countenance.

"Is that why you have been keeping to the cave?" he asked. "Because you don't want to freak out the kids?"

I nodded, solemnly.

"That," I said, "and because you keep bringing me bottles."

He had installed a miniature breaker box in the auxiliary quarters, and he was stripping back wires and screwing them into breakers and the return bar. I was testing them with a unit that lit up a certain way when I plugged it in, if he got it right. It was one of the few times we could talk, while we worked, with no saws or drills humming.

"Which one gets left behind?" Henry said. "This body, or that one?"

"You won't be able to tell the difference soon," I shrugged.

Henry flipped a breaker, and I plugged in the tester.

"Good," I said.

I moved across the room, talking while I did.

"More importantly," I continued, "the system won't be

able to tell the difference. I'll be you, as far as the system can tell."

Plugging the tester in once more, I nodded.

"Good here, too," I said. "I'll take on your soul's story, its debts and its credits, until I ring in the next person. That body will be left behind..."

I pointed at him, while I knelt at the last outlet.

"And this body will continue in its place," I finished.

The lights lit up, when I plugged it in; I angled this body so he couldn't see, and looked over its shoulder with a frown.

"Reversal," I said.

Henry's brow furrowed, his eyes narrowing.

"What?" he demanded.

I grinned.

"Just kidding, buddy," I said. "You can still tell a black wire from a white one. Good job."

He nodded, giving me a little grunt to show that my joke wasn't funny. While he screwed the cover on the breaker box, Henry pressed me further.

"Does it always work that way?" he said. "Do you always keep the body that you're in, and change it to resemble the other?"

I shrugged.

"I don't know," I said. "My memory is not so good, remember?"

With the cover completely screwed on, Henry closed the box and nodded at it with satisfaction. He turned, in place, and smiled.

"That would mean you do have a body," he said. "You keep changing it, but it's still the same body. The question then becomes where did that body come from?"

He pointed at me, and I shrugged again.

"I don't know," I repeated.

"Is that why you're called a ringer, maybe?" he said. "Did you bring some body back to life, to begin this journey you're on?"

I shook my head.

"Of course," I said, "resurrection used to be a much more common thing. When bodies were buried, not long ago, they were not drained of their fluids before being put in a box. Subsequently, some of those people woke up and clawed at the inside of their coffins trying to get out. When this was discovered, a mechanism was invented to alert folks above the ground that the person below the ground was not as dead as they had thought. This mechanism did include a bell, but that isn't where the term 'ringer' comes from."

Henry laughed.

"I know that," he said. "And the 'dead' in 'dead ringer' doesn't refer to death. It means 'exact', in this case; like, 'you're dead right' or 'that's dead on'. You already went off about how bodies have to be burned or drained after someone dies, to keep resurrection to a minimum. Actually, you have gone off about it a few times. Don't you remember?"

I searched this body's mind, while he tested the lights. It could have been gone because I am a ringer, or because I had been a few drinks deep at the time; either way, I didn't remember. I shook my head.

"A dead ringer is an exact duplicate," I said. "That's all I know. Not where I'm going, or where I'm coming from. That being said, I still don't like the term."

All the lights worked, and Henry turned to put his full attention on me. He spoke excitedly, and I couldn't help but catch it a little.

"Don't you see?" he said. "That's what I mean. You had to start somewhere, with your own body. Maybe your own karma was such that you had to do this for awhile. You might go back to a normal life, any time. Isn't that possible?"

"Don't say that word," I said. "I hate that word."

"What?" Henry arched an eyebrow. "Karma?"

I shuddered, and looked down at the device in this body's hand.

It was a little disappointing not to have seen the tester verify something as being wrong; it made me want to ask him to rewire something backwards, to test the tester.

"You know those folks," I said, instead, "that say 'anything is possible?'"

Henry nodded, grinning.

"They're wrong," I said. "They're also mortal. One leads to the other, when it comes to drawing conclusions about the system. I'm not mortal, Henry. I never have been. That's not how these things work."

I nudged him, to see him smile.

"I thought you were concerned about your body," I said. "Not mine. The body your kids and wife bury will be yours, buddy. It may not always be the case, but it will be this time."

XXXVI.

The last thing we needed to do was paint, and Henry thought it was okay to drink while whitening the walls. After the first bottle is gone, I scurry back inside to grab another.

In my defense, and Henry's, the first bottle had not started full.

I bring more than the bottle, setting a crumpled paper bag on the rung of a ladder before using both of this body's hands to open and pour. The little fridge in the unit is working, and the miniature ice cubes put out by the tray that come with it are perfectly scotch-sized.

With ice in both glasses, I set mine on the rung beside the bag, to pick it up. I open it, and Henry pays me no mind when I do. This body's fingers count one hundred dollar bill, then two and three. I take them out, fold them and put them in my pocket.

Right next to my phone, which hasn't buzzed in days.

I hand Henry the bag.

"Here you go, buddy," I say, with a solemn nod.

He takes it, and looks inside.

"I don't need this," he says, handing it back. "I'll be dead soon."

I refused to take it, turning away and stepping back.

"Two days is a long time," I said, "and you know that

your soul will be fine, no matter what you do. Why don't you cut loose, and drop the puritan act for awhile? It's your last chance, in this lifetime."

Henry shook his head.

"It's not an act," he said. "I do the things that feel natural to me, and most rewarding. Violating who I am on my way out would not feel liberating; it would feel like a betrayal."

I took him by the shoulders, although he was pressing the bag against this body's chest. A little shake got him laughing, and I joined in.

"Lighten up, man," I chuckled. "I have to be you soon."

Henry turned away, put the bag on the rung next to the bottle.

"Give it to Stephanie, then," I said. "I know she's going to be well taken care of, but extra cash is never a bad thing. Tell her it's strictly for pleasure, since you know she won't use the money you leave to do anything but take care of the kids."

He didn't respond, which I took as I good thing. After a few minutes he nodded, and smiled; which I took to mean 'okay' and 'thank you'.

I nodded back, to say 'you're welcome'.

"Where will you go?" he asked. "What will you do, with my body?"

I shrugged.

"I've always wanted to be a beach bum," I said. "Either that, or I did it before and liked it so much that the memory stuck with me somehow. I was thinking Santa Cruz, or Venice Beach."

He shook his head, poured himself a touch more scotch and another generous dram for me. I had finally started to notice that Henry was always more forthcoming with the booze when he wanted answers. If the answers didn't suit him, the whisky flowed even more freely. It made being withholding more rewarding than ever, so far as I couldn't remember.

"Not Santa Cruz," he said. "I used to spend a lot of time there in the summers, and I went to school there. People will recognize you."

I smiled, sipped.

"Oh, yeah?" I said. "What kind of people?"

He poured me more, until I had to drink to keep it from spilling.

"I'm serious, Ring," he said. "You better head to Venice, if you're going to be a beach bum. Stay away from Santa Cruz."

There was no more danger of my drink sloshing over the sides of my glass, but I didn't stop him from pouring more.

"I won't remember this conversation," I pointed out.

The words were a little soft around the edges, so I made sure to point out what I thought should be obvious.

"Not because you've been plying me with scotch," I clarified. "But because I'll be ringing you in soon."

I pulled the phone from my pocket, and was finally unsurprised to see it had a full charge. This body's fingerprint still opened it, which would have cast suspicion over the device if I already didn't trust it: I was more like Henry now than whoever I used to be, and this was definitely not his phone. Opening an app and pressing a facsimile of a button, I smile.

"Go ahead," I say. "Tell me what I need to do."

Henry looks at me, confused. Then he looks at the phone.

"Or," I amend, "what I need to not do."

He glances at me again, and nods.

"Don't go to Santa Cruz," he says. "No matter how tempted you may be. It's still winter. Venice Beach is the place for you."

I laughed, at the way he phrased it, and tapped the phone to stop the recording.

"There," I said. "I'm sure that will do the trick. Now, how about some more of that scotch?"

Henry laughed.

"Alright," he said, "but you're done painting. You were already only doing an adequate job, and all your skills go seriously downhill when you start to slur."

"I'm not slurring," I slurred, holding out the empty glass.

"Besides," I added, mostly coherent, "you did this on purpose. You always make it a point to get me good and liquored up when you want some answers. Admit it."

He filled the glass, and I drank more.

"I'll admit it," he said. "If you'll admit that you don't exactly put up a fight, even when you know that's what I'm doing."

I held up the remaining contents of my glass, and grinned.

"Cheers," I slurred.

XXXVII.

It turned out that he wasn't done pressing me for answers, and it was still awhile until dinner. We had built a little kitchen that spilled over into the even smaller dining room, and we sat on stools at the island after he covered all the paint supplies.

"Ring," he said, "there's something I've been meaning to ask you about. Something that I need a straight answer on."

The bottle is close enough for me to keep my own glass full, without reaching across him. I fill it, smiling.

"I don't do straight answers, Henry," I say. "You know that."

He laughs, but there is little humor in it.

"What happens to my soul?" he says. "While you're out there, representing me, what am I doing? I can't move on, can I?"

No matter how many times I sip, the questions still hang there.

"Well," I say, as gently as I can, "you'll be waiting, essentially. Your soul will go offline, for that period of time."

His eyes went wide.

"You mean, like..." he hesitated. "Like purgatory?"

I laughed.

"No," I said. "Like any of the other periods during

which a soul waits. Between one incarnation and another, whether it's on to Heaven or Hell or right here on good old Earth, souls tend to do a lot of waiting. Everything has to be just right, after all, to link a body with a soul and not have things go horribly awry. There's a lot of waiting involved, in all of that; your soul will feel right at home. You might even say that most souls feel more comfortable with waiting than they do with living."

Henry shook his head, joined me in a drink.

"So much for straight answers," he muttered.

"What do you want?" I countered. "You want me to put your soul's life into a context you can understand? There's no tropical paradise for you to vacation in, there in the between life; it's more like waiting in line. If I wanted to blow smoke, I'd tell you it will be wonderful. It won't. It will be kind of dull, and completely uneventful."

Henry laughed, finally loosening up a bit.

"The 'between life', huh?" He was still smiling. "What's that?"

I echoed his laughter, and it sounded much the same.

"Better to ask," I said, "what is the afterlife? Or the before life? Does the afterlife have an afterlife? If so, isn't it just a life in between lives? Is there nowhere for the soul to go, after it goes to the place it goes when the body dies? Can even Heaven be so great, that there is nothing better to reach for? And how great is that, to have nothing more ever be possible to you? How heavenly is it, to exist forever in an unchanging state?"

"Whoa, buddy," Henry nudged me. "I think you've had a bit too much."

He nodded at the bottle, as if the black label was not one of the few pure pleasures for a soul in any state.

"I disagree," I said, taking special care not to slur. "Why

do you think about what comes after this, instead of what comes before?"

Henry frowned.

"I don't know," he said. "I guess where we're going is more important than where we came from."

"Is it?" I snapped.

I was doing so good, with the slurring, I rewarded myself with another long string of sips. Despite his earlier observation, Henry topped off the drink as soon as I set it down.

"Maybe where we come from is the most important part," I said. "Maybe we have to figure out where we started, if we are to get where we are going. Does is not bother you that your memory is as bad as mine, when you think back to before you were born?"

His nod was slow, and thoughtful.

"Yeah, sure," he said. "You don't even have to go that far back, actually. I don't remember much of anything clearly from before puberty, and the first years after that are kind of a distant blur."

"Right?" I said. "That change was only slightly less dramatic than the next one you're facing, you know. You may be able to recall specific memories from before that big change, but good luck telling me what it actually felt like to be you back then. That's how it will be, in the between life."

Henry decided to start keeping up, as we were nearing the end of the bottle. He poured us both a round, while I added a touch of bitterness to my brightly colored commentary.

"I ought to know, you know," I said. "I live entirely in between."

"Why can't I just be a beach bum?" he asked, suddenly. "Why can't I do whatever you're planning to do, and change the direction of my soul appropriately? Why does it have to be you, in my body?"

"Would you?" I laughed. "Could you? Do you see yourself being able to forget Stephanie, and the kids, and your life? You'd break down in a week, and come back. Even if you didn't, you would be a shell in a couple months. You can't do that, either. It has to be this way, buddy."

Henry sighed, heavily.

"I know," he said. "It's natural to fight it, right?"

I shrugged.

"Did you fight puberty?" I said.

"No." Henry shook his head. "I also didn't have some weird dude come live with me for a few weeks, to get me acclimated to the thought of life as I know it ceasing to exist."

I threw back the rest of my drink.

"Well," I said, "maybe you should have."

XXXVIII.

We probably would have stood there the rest of the day, admiring our own handiwork, after everything was finally finished. First we walked around inside, to make sure we didn't overlook any important details; then we walked slow circles around it, commenting every few steps on some aspect of the build or our time together. Henry laughed when he remembered the finger in the grass, and how cooly Stephanie had ground it to nothing in the garbage disposal. Although it had been a hard time, and a challenging project, he seemed glad to have been through both.

"I think you might be wrong, buddy," he said, kindly enough. "I think maybe your soul has a path and a purpose, as well."

The doorjamb has a smear of dirt or mud, at waist level; it couldn't be bigger than a dime. I rub at it with the cuff of this body's flannel, and nod its head.

"Of course you do," I say. "You're mortal, and that makes sense from a mortal perspective. From an eternal point of view, it makes a lot more sense to dump those memories on a regular basis, even on a soul level. It is attachments that make people grow old, digging their pleasurably painful little hooks into their bodies to inevitably drag them into the ground. A ringer has no attachments, long-term. It's impossible, and thus so is the aging that comes with those attachments."

Henry laughed, more carefree than I had heard in days.

"What a load of crap," he said, still with kindness. "You really don't know what you're talking about, do you? When you don't know what you're talking about, you should just say 'I don't know what I'm talking about, by the way'. It would help clear things up, or keep them properly muddled."

I shrugged.

"I don't know what I'm talking about," I said. "By the way."

Henry looked me up and down; at this point, it must have been much like looking in a mirror that refused to mimic your actions. Other than our clothes, we were pretty much the same guy by now.

I was wearing his clothes, of course; they fit this body better, now. They weren't the exact same clothes, though.

That would have just been weird.

"You keep talking about bodies going in the ground," Henry pointed out. "You know I'm being cremated, right?"

I let this body's jaw drop, and its eyes go round.

"No, Henry!" I clutched him. "You can't! You have to bury it!"

To his credit, he lifted an eyebrow skeptically. It was too much for me to play it straight, and I started giggling a little maniacally.

"I don't know what I'm talking about, by the way," I repeated, between giggle fits. "It doesn't matter what happens to your body, buddy. The soul has completely lost interest by the time you burn or bury it."

Another circle round the structure, and our mutual congratulations came to an end at last. Stephanie stepped from the back door, stood in the grass and applauded us quietly.

"Looking good, boys," she said.

Her eyes went back and forth between us, and settled at last on Henry. It was both gratifying and very strange, to have her in on this.

"Ready for refreshments?" she said. "Lemonade? Iced tea?"

I laughed, and she looked my way.

"How about iced scotch?" I said.

Henry shook his head, stepped toward her and took her hand.

"Not tonight, Ring," he said.

They were looking in each other's eyes, and I put it together.

"Of course," I said. "I'll go inside."

Moving away from Henry, while still holding his hand, Stephanie took a half step toward me. She was shaking her head.

"No, Ring," she said. "Not yet."

Any other day, she would have been just as affectionate with him. She would have stood beside him, or near him, and they would have looked comfortable together in the most sincere way. They often touched each other, when they were close; and today was neither an exception to the rule nor an opportunity for an exceptionally clingy display. Holding hands, they exchanged the same kind of look they always did.

"Lemonade?" she asked, like she knew his answer.

Henry nodded, smiled at her smile.

"Yeah," he said. "Please."

He watched her walk back inside, and it wasn't like he was watching a beautiful woman or a snazzy car pass by. From the look on his face, Henry may well have been watching a sunset. I was so busy not being touched by the simple sublime expression, I only peripherally noticed that Stephanie had come back out. He watched her as she returned, the same way, and bright colors swirled about them both as they came near each other once more.

"Ring."

Stephanie was taking to me, and I was staring all dreamily at Henry.

I coughed, turned, and smiled.

"Yeah?"

It was then that I noticed what she was holding, and that she was proffering it proudly to me. When this body's eyes came into focus on the blue label, I snatched the bottle from her with a quiet whoop.

"Hey, alright!" I said. "Is this for me?"

She laughed, took Henry's hand again. I could still see their colors, and I delighted in their warm reds and yellows and greens almost as much as I did my new blue.

"It's for you," she said. "Henry said that you understood about him being with us tonight, and that you planned to hole up until this is all over. I thought it might be nice to do you a solid, since you've done us so many."

Stephanie watched me open it, and sniff carefully. When she laughed at me, both Henry and I joined in.

"Also," she said. "Henry gave me the money. Thanks, Ring, really. You're right, it will help. I'm glad you convinced him to take it. I'm also glad that you did not convince him to do anything crazy with it while he had the chance."

All of us exchanged looks then, as I hovered this body's nose over the sublime scent wafting from the open bottle. I smiled, at each of them.

"It was a test, you know," I said. "Henry passed, with flying colors."

Henry shot me a dark look, which was actually mostly put on, and laughed.

"Also," I added, "I have no idea what I'm talking about."

XXXIX.

We walked around the mother-in-law unit one last time, this time with Stephanie trailing the same slow path. She paid us both a lot of compliments, and avoided looking at this body too much; I accepted graciously, and understood completely. I made sure to avoid saying that Henry did all the work, since it looked like there were two of him instead of one of each of us; but I did find more tactful ways to give him the lion's share of the credit.

It does belong to him, after all.

Once we complete the circuit, and the conversation drifts to how soon one of their actual mothers-in-law might be staying here, I step away. A few more steps, and I'm near the back door. When I turn back to look, one last time, they're both watching me. A smile is playing about Stephanie's lips, and I can't miss the sadness in it. She calls out, softly.

"Not yet, Ring," she says, again.

Henry nods, and crosses the space between us in a few careful strides. I like the way he inhabits his body, and can't help but hope I do it the same level of justice.

As he gets close, Henry throws his arms wide and wraps them around me. For a moment, I'm lost in his colors and warmth; then I smile, and return the embrace.

I resist the urge to cry, and the urge to examine the urge.

Stephanie is right behind him, and her sweet flowery scent overwhelms me in a whole different way. Before I can be tempted to bury my face in her hair or her shoulder, and sob like a baby, I remind myself that I am not Henry and Henry is not me.

I disengage, and this body's eyes are dry.

The whole time, I've been holding the bottle she gave me. With the cork back in it, the smell is no longer tickling this body's nostrils; that doesn't mean I'm not acutely conscious of the weight of it in this body's hand. I look down at it, and Henry laughs.

"Careful," he says. "Remember what you said about the danger of attachments. Don't let Johnny get his hooks in you."

The way I shake this body's head, I make sure he knows I'm not kidding. I keep its expression stern, and stoic, as I reply.

"This," I say, holding up the bottle, "is the perfect example of a healthy attachment. I'll consume it completely, enjoy it thoroughly, and forget it promptly. I won't belabor how quickly it goes, or mourn it when it has gone; I will live with it, in the moment, until it has left this world. Someday, the system willing, I'll have another just like it and do the same."

I give the bottle a most loving look, and Henry drops a bomb on me.

"They are actually discontinuing the blue label," he said. "It won't be so easy to find, soon. Enjoy it while you can."

This time, the dirty look I gave him was real.

"I'll forget you said that," I reminded him. "I'll forget about this bottle, and when they don't make it any more I'll forget that they ever did."

I didn't notice that I was clutching the bottle to this

body's chest, until Stephanie moved in for another hug. It was brief, and I was glad; whether she was sparing her feelings or mine, it was for the best. She breathed in my ear as I pulled away, and I smiled at her words.

"Thank you," she said. "You're a weird one, Ring; but thank you."

I shrugged, stretched this body's lips into a smile.

"Who wants to be normal?" I said.

Henry hugged me again, too; and this time it was me whispering in his ear. I didn't mean for it to sound spooky, or anything; but I suppose it might have.

"I'll see you later," I said.

He was nodding when we pulled apart, a mirror image separating from itself. One of us carried the weight of the world; and the other, a bottle of scotch. Although I wouldn't trade places with him for anything, I suppose that wouldn't stop me from doing it later.

No more words need to be spoken, just now. I go through the back door quietly, after one last glance at them together. A good long look inside my new heart tells me that the darkness has a solid floor now, and I'm comforted at the thought of lowering myself to its level by the end of the night. Soaking in the colors and lingering thoughts in Henry's man cave is both painful and sublime, and the pain goes away slowly as the contents of the bottle do.

Rather than read his books or watch his news, I simply sit with Henry's thoughts. I wonder if I'll be a wide-eyed optimist when he's gone, and if all my cynicism came with this body. It's a nice thought, but I'm pretty sure that's all it is. I've worked with the system for too long to ever hope my next body might be compelled to go skipping through any fields of daisies.

The dim glow from the inactive devices in the room are enough for me to see, while I'm so focused on the colors instead of the light. All I need is enough visibility to pour, and drink; those motions, at least, I can perform from memory. I don't know much about other immortals, but I have heard one thing about the lot of us: we do like to drink.

When the door opens, I hide my surprise. The hours have passed, the bottle is nearly empty, and Henry is standing in the doorway looking down at me. He flips on the light, and I hold out the bottle.

"Come in," I say. "Sit down. Have a drink."

XL.

Henry waved away the offer, and I poured the rest of the scotch into my glass. He motioned toward the refrigerator, still the considerate host.

"More ice?" he said.

I shook this body's head, annoyed. I wanted to yell at him, to stand up and poke him in the chest; to challenge him to do the impossible, and take me out before I could take him out. I wanted to watch him rage against the system, against the inevitable, and against me.

"Is it time?" he murmurs.

I throw back the rest of the drink, abandoning all decorum. It burns, going down, and I don't shut off the painful signal. Instead I turn it on full blast, and let myself stew in the network of searing sensations. A frown spreads across this body's face as the pain fades, and I let it settle in place. I put aside the empty glass, and turn to him.

"Just a moment," I whisper. "Just one more moment."

He laughs, and I feel the anger building again. How can he be so calm, when I am so overwrought? Why should he accept the very thing I rail against, or feel a measure of equanimity for every drop of my own agitation? Why am I the one reeling in discomfort, while he demonstrates such steely aplomb?

Aren't I him?

Where is my calm?

I meet his eyes, and frown.

"Write me a note, would you?" I say. "Tell me that I need to get out of here, now. After it's over, I won't remember anything. I'll be stinking drunk and most likely tempted to go ahead and pass out here. I need a clear sign, telling me I better get out of here. It wouldn't do to have the kids or Stephanie find us here together in the morning. It has to be you, just you. Did you empty your bowels, like I told you to?"

He laughs once more, and I almost grit this body's teeth at the sound.

"Gross, buddy," he says. "Yeah, I did."

"Stop being so damned jolly," I say. "You don't have long."

When he laughs this time, something melts inside of me. Rather than watching the anger build even more, I feel it begin to subside. The thing replacing it makes me feel soft, and vulnerable; that, I push away.

"Write me a note," I say, again. "Tell me to get out of here, now. Tell me I have money in my pocket, and that I should get out of here without taking anything more. Tell me to listen to my recordings to myself, after I get somewhere safe. They're on my phone. Hurry, do it now."

I was hoping he would resist, because of my demanding tone or my softening heart. He didn't, though; instead he went to a cabinet, opened it and removed a notebook. A pen was already nestled in the metal spiral, and he pulled it out and started writing on a blank page.

'RING,' he wrote, in bold capital letters, 'GET OUT OF HERE. DON'T TAKE ANYTHING BUT THE PHONE AND MONEY IN YOUR POCKET. WHEN YOU GET SOMEWHERE SAFE, LISTEN TO THE RECORDINGS ON YOUR PHONE.'

I nodded, only to stop and frown as he kept writing. The last line jumped out at me, as he pulled his hand away. I felt the anger start to mount again.

'I FORGIVE YOU, BUDDY," it said. 'YOU ARE LOVED.'

Henry fetched a stapler, from the same cabinet with all the notebooks. He placed the collar of his shirt between its jaws, along with the sheet of paper, and stapled the note to the material. It hung over his heart, that last line staring at me as frankly as I stared at it.

"That's just going to confuse me," I said. "I won't understand."

A slight smile on Henry's face told me he knew that, and didn't care.

He waited, the picture of patience. I felt this body begin to tremble, as I personified hesitation. We had one last long look at each other, and his smile grew almost imperceptibly.

"It's time," he says. "I can feel it."

I know this isn't usually how it goes, even if I can't remember how it ever went before. The only thing tearing me up more than not doing what I need to do is contemplating doing it, and then living with it. I run through every possibility that I've never considered in moments, standing there and staring at my body double.

Actually, he's the one standing there staring at his doppleganger; and the way that he's looking at me, and smiling, is enough fuel for me to finish what I need to do.

The ringing has reached its zenith pitch, while I lived comfortably and got so used to tuning it out. Henry's right, it is time. I look in his eyes and see that he is letting go already, and that making him hang on is causing him pain for the sake of putting off my own.

I stand, slowly, and spread this body's arms. One last embrace, from someone who calls me friend, before I step back into the loneliness that is my life. As soon as I feel the warmth of his body against me, I pull it all into me. The ringing increases in volume, until it is my whole world; then it stops, and he sags in this body's arms.

For a moment that seems it will last forever, we are both present together in a place without bodies or thought or darkness. I see everything, and I watch him see it all with me, and it feels as though we may melt into forever together in the most sublime fashion.

Out of the light, a darkness emerges. It swirls about us, and makes me keenly aware of our separateness. I push Henry away, with arms I don't have, and use them to wave away the darkness. The swirling surrounds me, and embraces me. At last, it soaks into me.

There is nothing now, but darkness.

XLI.

I hear the ringing right away, and sigh with the kind of relief only a ringer can know. It's so quiet, and distant, I know I get to be me for awhile this time. Of course, I don't remember how long I got to be me last time; but that doesn't matter, if I can't remember it.

For some reason, this body is lying on the floor next to the one I must have just finished ringing. I get a good look at his face, and am glad to see that his countenance is both peaceful and easy on the eyes. On this body's feet, I check the closest mirror to make sure the faces are the same.

At first, I think maybe this body needs glasses. I try to fashion its breathing around correcting that, only to be interrupted by an involuntary hiccup. It tastes of scotch, and I can't help but smile.

Well, I hope I had a good time.

A cabinet is standing open, with a stack of notebooks on one shelf and a couple bottles on the other. I smile again when I see the black label, and grab the closest bottle. While I'm sipping, without transferring the drink to a glass, I look down at the guy again. His shirt has a note pinned to it, and it has my name at the top.

I kneel, and pull at the sheet of paper. After reading the note, I look around and sip some more. The counter has a pen and an empty glass on it, and I seize both.

Right next to where whoever penned the missive wrote my name, I do the same. The handwriting is nearly identical, which means either I wrote it or the dead guy did. Probably the dead guy, with the weird part there at the end. I can't see why I'd write that, to myself.

If I hadn't thought I should read the note, after ringing him, I would have destroyed it; I know that. I'm sure there's no harm in taking the unopened bottle, along with the items in this body's pockets; and a nearby backpack to stow it in, so I'm not walking around homeless with an obviously open container. The backpack has another notebook, and a few pens; after careful consideration, I leave them in there. I stuff the note in an inside pocket, have a good last look at the jeans and flannel I've got on in the mirror, and stick this body's tongue out at its own reflection.

One slow look around the room makes me want to relax, even if just for a minute. I don't know where I'll go, only that I need to. I don't even know where I am, although geography really doesn't mean much to a ringer. The job is the same, in whatever feet you're using to walk on whatever patch of dirt you're treading.

The colors in the room are subtle, but comforting. It can't possibly hurt, for me to take a minute to get this body's breathing right. I need to be able to navigate, out of this place and to the next; and for some reason I got a bit too inebriated to move on right away despite the clear advice to get this body moving. Natural breathing only feels unnatural for a few breaths, and I close this body's eyes to better concentrate on turning the other into the one.

When I open them, a darkness is swirling about the discarded body. All of the colors in the room are muted by its motions, and its presence. I leap at it, and swipe this body's hand at it; the darkness envelopes the limb, only to swirl away and back toward the corpse.

I curse at it, finally. Raising this body's voice to a controlled shout, I level a string of powerful words at the floating fog. It swirls into a cyclone, and the miniature tornado of darkness turns in on itself until it disappears as quietly as it came.

Speaking of quiet...

The cursed shouting may have left me alone with the dead man again, but it cut my time to prepare for the next leg of my endless journey short. I check the pockets of this body's clothes one last time, and head for the only door in the room.

It opens onto a kitchen and dining area, which opens onto a living room large enough for several families to lounge in. Just as I spot the front door, I hear footsteps on the stairs. I bolt for it, and fumble with the locks for a second longer than I think I have. I don't look back as I slam the door behind me, and I'm across the street in someone else's yard before I see any lights come on.

The front door opens, and I watch from behind a friendly shrub. This body's vision is still swimming a little from the drink, and I have to wipe away the watery haze before I can see clearly.

By that time, the front door is closed and the porch is empty.

I sigh, still being cautious, and slip through the shadows in the direction of the lighted sky. More lights mean more people, and businesses that both close at nightfall and stay open late. That mix means plenty of places to hole up, and plenty of other people looking to hole up somewhere.

While I walk, I sling the backpack into this body's arms and fish the bottle out two or three times. I feel a silly grin trying to take hold, and am keenly aware of my reality of inhabiting a whole new body; so I try to keep it down. No need to wander the streets looking both drunk and ghastly.

All those lights are coming from Sunrise; the avenue, not the event. That won't happen for several hours now, and by then I will hopefully be sleeping off this excessive buzz as effectively as I'll be sleeping off the memory of who I used to be. I might even know what state I'm in.

Let's just hope no one is being where I want to be, tonight. Finding a place to put a body just because it's in my way can be so exhausting.

XLII.

One part of me thinks that I have always wanted to live on a beach, to soak up the culture and the ocean air for a stretch of time that seems to have no end. Another part of me wonders if maybe I lived that life once, and loved it so much that I will always long for it. No part of me questions the desire itself, and it seems only natural that the next few days see me making my way toward the ocean.

Without much cash, I had to walk to the bus station; something about Santa Cruz rang an impossible bell in my memory, and I had enough to buy the ticket for the long uncomfortable ride. From the next bus station, it was a few blocks through town and a bit more walking to reach the beach. I followed the smell of the ocean the whole way, and practiced a natural smile every time I passed a reflective surface.

I pulled the note I had written to myself out of my pocket several times during the journey, and even checked to make sure I had the phone. I didn't listen to the messages, though; that could wait at least a couple days, maybe even a week or two. The ringing was so faint, I knew I had plenty of time to take a free breath or two before I got back to work.

The temperatures were not ideal, which made sense when I found out that it was only just the beginning of

January. The year didn't matter, not really; it never does to a ringer.

Fortunately, the chill factor is only a factor if I want it to be, and the cold nights meant that I had the entire beach pretty much to myself. There was no need to nestle under the wharf, as long as I kept my breathing right or filled this body's belly with a black label blanket.

With so little cash, that wouldn't be an option much longer.

I wandered the boardwalk during the day, staring at the dancing translucent colors of the winter visitors that hung in the air and sitting on the steps of businesses that wouldn't open till summer. The rides seemed to think they would come alive at any moment, and sometimes I watched them to see if they would. They never did, though; and I stopped waiting.

The wharf was busier, and I should have known better than to frequent it. This time was for me, not for watching the thoughts of others take colorful shape around them. Since I don't so much need to eat, I didn't for the first couple days; I just walked all day, and slept under the stars at night. Everywhere I went, the ocean was always nearby.

Most of the dishes and prices advertised would put too big of a dent in the meager supply of cash I was carrying, but I finally gave in to the temptation presented by the glass case I kept passing. I was eating my fish tacos, and sipping a beer, when someone walking by stopped in their tracks to watch me.

"Henry?"

I keep eating, until I notice that she seems to be addressing me.

"Henry, how are you?"

She sits down, and the bite that had been in this body's mouth lodges itself in its throat as I try to swallow.

I shake this body's head, gulp audibly.

"Sorry," I say. "You have mistaken me for someone else."

Her face is pretty, even when it's twisted in confusion. It makes me wonder who this Henry guy was, and just how they knew each other.

It doesn't matter, of course; I know the rules.

I finish my beer in one giant slurp, and stand abruptly. I'm left looking down at her, and feeling bad for some reason. I make sure my next words have a dual message, by not hiding the irritation in this body's voice.

"It's okay," I say. "It happens all the time."

I walk away, throwing the rest of the food in the trash without breaking stride. I keep on walking, and don't stop until I find myself retracing my steps to the bus station. Before buying a ticket, I do what I should have done from the very beginning, or at least that first quiet night under the stars. I close this body's eyes, and focus completely on the distant sound of ringing. Information leaps at me, in clumps I don't understand, and this body twitches with the organic download.

I open this body's eyes, make my way to the counter and give the cashier my best and most practiced smile yet.

"I need to get to Venice Beach," I say, all happily. "One ticket to as close to Venice Beach as I can get."

I'm so giddy, I can't help but speak my next thought out loud. I don't care if she understands, or thinks I'm off; it's a bus station, after all.

"It looks like I'll be ringing in a summer."